# Murder Takes a Selfie

Shannon Symonds

SWEETWATER BOOKS
An imprint of Cedar Fort, Inc.
Springville, Utah

ISBN 13: 978-1-4621-3880-7

Published by Sweetwater Books, an imprint of Cedar Fort, Inc.
2373 W. 700 S., Springville, UT 84663
Distributed by Cedar Fort, Inc., www.cedarfort.com

Library of Congress Control Number: 2021936727

Cover design by Shawnda T. Craig


Printed in the United States of America

10 9 8 7 6 5 4 3 2 1

Printed on acid-free paper

*To my mother, Beverly Sappenfield, who has listened to every word I've ever written. You may be losing your sight, but you've never lost your vision. Thank you for teaching us anything is possible.*

# Contents

# 1

# Contrary to Popular Belief

"So why can't I come to your mom's wedding again?" Sophie asked.

Esther pushed her glasses up her nose and, feeling warm, undid the top button of her sweater as she thought about the question. She locked the Oceanside High library money box in the desk drawer and put the key in a coffee cup where anyone could steal it but wouldn't. It was one of the things Esther loved about their small town.

"She said they want to keep it small, just family and Hart's partner at work, Officer Ironpot," Esther said as she packed her AP chem book in her backpack. "I think the whole wedding is kind of a mess." Esther wiped her pencil shavings off the library desk and into a trash can.

"Wait. Officer Ironpot is just a co-worker. I'm your best friend. Don't I outrank him?" Sophie pushed the book cart behind the desk and started turning off lights in the ancient library. "And what are you going to call Officer Hart? Dad?"

"No! I have no idea," Esther said loudly enough that she looked over her shoulder to be sure they were truly alone in the usually quiet library. Oceanside High's library was dedicated in 1896. It was dusty and old, but Esther loved it, right down to the unused fireplace.

"What's his first name?" Sophie called from across the room while she turned off a light.

"Joe." Another light went off.

Sophie came back and got her coat off the rack. "Isn't it weird to have your mom get married so soon after he proposed? Wasn't it only a few weeks ago?" She put her books into her backpack. After hefting the huge pack onto her petite frame, she pulled her long black hair out from under the straps and cleaned her round glasses. At four-foot-eleven, the pack was almost as big as she was.

"It's fast. I mean, they're friends and worked together for years, but I just met him last fall." Esther put her own backpack on.

"So why the rush?"

Esther smiled at Sophie. "I asked Grandma Mable why, and she told me there was no reason to procrastinate happiness. But I heard the pastor at church tell my mom to beat the devil by running to the altar. Do you think it's odd that when I was little I always wanted my real father to come back and be with us?"

"He came back all right." Sophie laughed. "And then you had to call nine-one-one. He's crazy mean. Did your mom tell you your dad was in prison before he escaped?"

"You know, we had good days too. He wasn't always mean." Sophie's questions stung. Esther and her mom had moved with Grandma Mable to Oregon when Esther was nine, but she still remembered some of the good days. "We never talked about him very much."

"I've known you since you moved here. You never talked about him at all."

"It's like I said, we were in hiding, until he walked away from a work release program last month and found us. Besides, he said he was sorry before they took him back to prison to finish his sentence" *Why am I defending him? I need to grow up and let go of childish dreams.*

The last bell rang. The hallway outside the library filled with noisy students getting on buses or going to track practice.

The library door opened, and Parker Stuart came in laughing with Ashley Gates Cadeau, one of the prettiest girls in Esther's sophomore class. Esther let Sophie take the desk while she pretended to be busy organizing books. *Of course he's with her. She looks as if she could wear two drinking straws for jeans. She should be a brunette hair model for shampoo commercials starring Parker, a handsome Viking who buys his clothes at REI.* Esther pushed her glasses into place.

"Hello. Is it too late to check out a book?" Parker asked with his British accent. Ashley smiled at him as if he were the only person in the room.

"We just closed everything up," Sophie said.

Esther looked up just in time to catch Sophie looking back and giving her a knowing look—one eye narrowed and her mouth twisted in a half-smile. Parker leaned on the library desk, letting a lock of his blond hair fall out of his ponytail and into his face.

Parker had recently come to Oceanside High from England with his twin sister, and everything about him gave Esther butterflies. He hung out with Nephi, her seventeen-year-old uncle, and had even come to her house once, but she was too shy to speak to him.

"Oh. It's all good." He shrugged and turned to go.

"Wait!" Sophie called him back. "Esther can help you."

Esther gave Sophie a wide-eyed look. Sophie just smiled and stepped back.

Parker stood up. "That's okay. I can do it Monday. I need to go run with the long distance track team anyway." He gave Esther a smile. "Thanks."

Ashley stepped even closer to him and followed him out the door.

"Sophie!" Esther turned on her friend, shaking her head.

"What? You know you like him. Every time he walks by you comment on what he's wearing."

Esther smiled. "It's just his accent. He's smart and, well, I like his sweaters."

"Right, it's the sweaters." Sophie laughed. "Let's tell the librarian good night and then go study on the beach."

"Sounds perfect." Happy to change the subject, Esther peeked into the librarian's office. "Good night, Ms. Priest."

The young librarian looked up at Esther and smiled. "Good night, girls. Are you going to the midnight book launch and signing during spring break?"

"Of course," Sophie said.

"I thought so." Ms. Priest gave Sophie a beautiful smile. "If I don't see you there, I'll see you after spring break."

Esther loved working in the library with Ms. Priest and Sophie. It was a great place to do her homework, and library sciences gave her an excuse to study for her college entrance exams.

The girls walked through the library to the double doors and pushed them open together. Esther turned around and made sure they had locked the doors behind them. They stood for a moment on the cement stairs, watching students drive out of the parking lot. In the distance, she could see the river flowing into the ocean. A gust of wind freed some of Esther's brown hair from her ponytail.

Adjusting her backpack, Esther said, "Come on, let's go to the beach."

✦ ✦ ✦

Esther and Sophie walked along the riverbank until they reached the road to Esther's house. They passed her house and walked one more block to the beach.

The northern Oregon beach had an old swing set and a picnic table hidden in the grassy dunes near the beach access road. It was the perfect spot to study when the weather was good.

"Is this where they're having the ceremony?" Sophie got out her books and spread out next to Esther, facing the surf. "I bet it'll be a beautiful day, and I won't be there."

"I think so," Esther said. "All I know is Grandma Mable bought me bedazzled flip flops. They're straight out of the nineties and I love them. She bought my Uncle Nephi new Converse for his suit."

"How can he be your uncle?"

"Grandma calls him her best surprise." Esther laughed. "I think he is her smelliest."

"Speak of the stink, here he comes." Sophie pointed toward the beach access.

The entire long distance track team was headed their way. Paisley Pamela Stuart's long, perfect legs had the social-media queen ahead of the pack.

Paisley passed a middle-aged man in a sweat suit leaving the beach, and her lipstick fell out of her hot pink shorts. By the time the man picked up her lipstick and turned to give it to her, Paisley had passed Esther in a cloud of perfume, running toward the ocean.

Paisley's twin, Parker, was red faced and breathing hard as he ran toward them, racing to catch up. Nephi was right behind Parker.

Esther sighed deeply. Her stomach fluttered and her hands shook as she nervously twisted hair that had fallen out of her ponytail.

Laughing, Sophie said, "You've got it bad."

"I do not!" She hid her nervous hands in her lap but let out a quiet laugh.

"Yes, you do."

"I respect his mind. Have you heard him in lit class? He recites. For an athlete, he's brilliant."

"Right," Sophie said. "You were thinking about his mind."

"Quiet. Here he comes," Esther said. Parker spotted her and Sophie in their usual spot and nodded.

Nephi saw her. "Hey, geek squad! Are you checking out my manly legs?"

"You're going to blind someone!" Sophie yelled. Then she looked at Esther, and a slow smile spread across her face. "You like Parker. Too bad he's a twin to the mean girl."

# 2

# One Big Happy Family

The roar of the Pacific Ocean made it hard to hear the wedding ceremony. Ominous clouds rolled across the steel gray sky. Esther's beautiful mother, Grace James, stood beside Officer Joseph Hart on a grass-covered dune, facing the sea and clutching a handful of daisies.

Their aging pastor held a Bible open in one hand and tried to push his comb-over back into place with his other hand as the salt air blew. His lips were moving and he was obviously talking, but the wind was so loud Esther heard only a few words.

On the horizon, storm clouds dumped rain in sheets of water across the ocean. The gale violently whipped the bride's long white dress and pushed the rain toward the small wedding party.

By the time Esther's mother kissed Hart and the pastor pronounced them man and wife, heavy raindrops were falling. Grace threw her head back and opened her mouth to catch the rain and then fell into Hart's arms, laughing. Holding each other, they became drenched in the waist-high beach grass.

Esther wanted to be happy for her mom. But she couldn't while her father was in prison. It felt odd, like a betrayal.

Her throat swelled and she couldn't swallow. Not only had her parents' marriage ended when her mom had left her dad years ago, but it had ended in violence that sent him to prison. And it was all her fault.

The spring storm picked up. The wind plucked a daisy that was tucked into the fishtail braid in her long brown hair. Waves churned up black sand, pounding the Oregon coast.

Beaming, her mother turned to her, her grandmother, her little sister, Mary, Nephi, and Nephi's foster sister, Hope, triumphantly waving her bouquet in the air. Petals from the flowers blew away, leaving bald stalks in a ribbon. Hart gave her another kiss, and his friend, Officer Ironpot, began playing the bagpipes. Still, Esther couldn't remember a time her mother had been this happy, and Hart seemed sweet.

The wedding was planned so quickly Esther didn't have time to get used to the idea of her mother with someone else. The thought of another man, other than her father, living in their house made her head hurt. *What if he walks around in his pajamas? I'm going to be sick.*

Esther overheard her mother and her grandmother laughing about the pastor pushing them to get married before there were any *shenanigans.*

Ironpot continued to play the bagpipes. He was dressed up like a highlander, complete with a kilt. Esther couldn't look away from his desperate attempts to hold down his flapping kilt until Mary, her seven-year-old sister, tugged at her sleeve.

"What is it, Mary?"

"I'm cold," she whined. The little flower girl was shaking so hard, rose petals were falling out of her dainty white basket.

"Me too. As cold as ice cream." Smiling, Esther gathered Mary's thin body in, holding her close, loving her curly redheaded sister. She looked so much like her Grandma Mable. "Just a few more minutes."

Then she saw something odd. The sea grass was moving together in the wind, except behind the bride and groom. Just a little to the side and a few yards behind them, the grass was shaking like something was moving it. Then, between the blades of grass, Esther saw the top of a head with black hair, parted neatly in the middle. Just as she realized who was in the grass, her best friend's head popped up and swiveled as if she was checking her location, round glasses looking frantically right and left, tight braids swinging, before dropping down.

*What is she doing? I can't . . . No, I can totally believe it.*

The movement in the grass grew closer.

"Sophie," she hissed. "Sophie, what are you doing?"

Sophie's head popped up, and she gave Esther a sheepish grin before she ducked again.

Esther took a step toward her friend, when she felt a hand on her shoulder and turned around to see her Grandma Mable.

"It's like watching Ken and Barbie," Grandma said.

"Huh?" Esther asked.

"Ken and Barbie—your mom and your new stepdad," Grandma Mable said in her gravelly voice while pointing at her mom and Hart.

"Stepdad?" Shocked, Esther echoed her grandmother.

"That's right. What are you going to call him? Officer Dad?" The wind blew Mable's laughter away, pulling red and gray curls from her messy bun.

Esther stepped between Mable's line of vision and Sophie, folding her arms nervously.

Grandma Mable was as tough as nails—rusty nails. Her right eyebrow raised, giving Esther a look that said she knew exactly what was going on. Mable leaned dramatically to the side to look past Esther and pointed at Sophie.

But Esther was distracted. Over Mable's shoulder, she saw Nephi's tall and lanky frame waving at her. He was acting like a monkey, playing charades and gesturing something in her direction. *What is he trying to . . . ?*

"Grandma!" Nephi waved both arms. "We need pictures."

"Grandma, where's your cell phone?" Esther said.

"Here. Good thing it's waterproof." Grandma traded the phone for what was left of Esther's bridesmaid bouquet.

Esther began snapping pictures. First of the bride and groom still talking to their little gray-haired pastor. Then a snap of Ironpot, with his big belly, trying to protect his bagpipes by putting them inside his tight jacket. She took a picture of his knees and garters showing under the kilt and laughed to herself.

Hope had been holding the guitar she was playing for the ceremony until the rain started. But she was prepared. She was tucking her guitar into a black garbage bag when Esther took her photo.

Ironpot's wife was a few feet away from the group. She clearly did not have on waterproof mascara, and the careful curls in her dark hair were washing away in the mist. Her little boy was pounding on her leg, trying to get her attention. She took a picture of them.

To Esther's horror, Ironpot's son gave up on his mother and found Sophie, who was trying to wave him away.

"Hey!" Esther called. "We need to take pictures." No one heard her but Uncle Nephi. He gave a shrill whistle, getting everyone's attention.

He held his arms up and shouted over the storm, "Guys! We want to get some pics to remember this moment."

Grace laughed and shook her head. Esther knew her mom hated having her picture taken. It was a big no-no during the years they hid from her father. Her mother was a pro at avoiding cameras.

"We can do it later," her mom said.

"No way, Grace," Hart said. "Everyone gather around."

They all lined up on top of the dune and looked at Esther.

"Wait!" her mom said. "Esther, you need to be in the picture."

"I hate pictures, Mom. Besides, who will take it?" She wasn't sure yet that this was a memory she wanted to save. Her thin fingers were so cold she couldn't hold the camera still. She looked at Hart on the screen. *What if he's like Dad? Will I make him mad too?*

"I'll take it!" Her best friend's head popped up out of the nearby grass. Sophie adjusted her round glasses and stood up. Everyone began laughing. "What? I didn't want to miss it. Okay, I'm not family but, hey, how often does your best friend's mom get married?"

Sophie ran to Esther, gave her a quick hug, and took the camera.

"I am so glad you're here, Soph," Esther said. The sight of Sophie's silly smile lifted Esther's tension.

"Yeah? Well, get in the picture." She gave Esther a little push. Esther lined up with the others and held Mary's hand.

Sophie held up the phone and motioned them to get closer. "Okay, everyone. Say cheese!"

Esther's family immediately made bizarre faces. Esther stuck her tongue out, and Mary made her favorite monkey face and pulled her ears out. Then they all laughed.

"What just happened?" Sophie asked.

"You said cheese!" Mary said and the whole group did it again. By now everyone was into the game and laughing.

"Okay, okay!" Nephi bellowed. "Can we just get one good picture? Really? Can we be serious for one minute?"

"Who's the girl you want to send the picture to, Nephi?" Grandma Mable asked, setting off a new round of giggles.

"Paisley," Esther said in a snarky voice and gave Nephi a little push.

"Okay, okay," her mom said, hands in the air. "We can do this! Smile, everyone, and try to act normal."

Sophie took several pictures and then showed them to Esther's mom.

"Perfect," her mom said. "Now let's save these for posterity and get out of the rain."

"Okay," Nephi said, "But send me the pictures."

✦ ✦ ✦

The wedding party left the sandy beach. Laughing, they trotted toward Esther's house, soaked, cold, and happier than they had been in a long time.

She could see the roof of their old Victorian with odd angles, gables, and a large round turret over the top of the pine trees that surrounded it. It sat a block off the beach. They talked and laughed about the spring rain as they walked the sidewalk and narrow road through the pines.

Esther rounded the corner. Police cars were parked all around the house.

The police chief stood on the wide wrap-around porch, arms resting on his duty belt under a banner that read, "Congratulations!" Aviator sunglasses, handlebar mustache, and his flat expression gave nothing away. The front door opened, and half the police force and their wives came onto the porch and shouted, "Surprise!"

Grace froze, but Hart ran up the stairs and began slapping his buddies' backs. Necanicum City police officers and their families crowded around Grace and hugged her.

Esther heard the chief tell her mom that Ironpot had been in on their surprise from the beginning. Then Ironpot blew a sour note on his bagpipes and everyone quieted down and turned to the chief.

"As you know," the chief began, "Hart and Grace wanted this to be a quiet family affair. Well, we are one big happy law-enforcement family. And we can't have you joining our family without celebrating it, so the team put together a little gift for you." He turned and motioned to Ruby, a dispatcher. She handed him an envelope.

He went on. "We all pitched in and bought you a two-and-a-half-week honeymoon vacation in Hawaii. You'll be staying in Dylan's time share."

Her mother covered her open mouth and suppressed a squeal while Hart grinned and started thanking his friends, who shook his hand and slapped his back.

The chief held one hand up to quiet the celebrating and went on. "Mable helped me, and we made arrangements for you to fly out tomorrow. And even though we want every officer in the house working during spring break, you are off the hook. So! Plan to work Christmas Day. Congratulations, Mr. and Mrs. Joseph Hart!"

Esther's family and the police force melted into one big joyful celebration, hugging and congratulating the couple.

# 3

# The Apple Doesn't Fall Far from the Tree

Esther's cat—Molly for short, named for the unsinkable Molly Brown who survived the *Titanic*—walked on the laptop keyboard, looked at the blank screen, and flicked her tail in Esther's face.

"Are you making fun of me, Miss Molly? What would you write? The assignment is what I did during my spring break."

The cat lay on the keyboard, making random numbers appear on the computer, and looked at Esther. She was sure Molly was looking down her nose at her.

"How's this for a first line? 'This spring break, in the wettest wedding of the century, my mother married the cop that rescued us from my father's kidnapping attempt, and now I have a new stepfather. I still don't know what to call him—Hart, Stepdad, Hey You.' Or maybe I could report on hours of study with Sophie and helping Grandma babysit my little sister. My life is either so boring it would put the class to sleep or such a mess, I would die if anyone found out about it."

Molly began licking her nether region.

"I agree. It's nothing to write about, much less share with the public. So, what would you write?"

Esther's desk sat under the window in the turret of the old house. Her bedroom was on the top floor. Just beyond the trees she could see the moonlight sparkle on the ocean. Usually, she loved writing at her antique desk, with the sound of the ocean blowing in on the breeze, but not today.

She was staring out the window when her cell phone rang, interrupting her thoughts. It was Sophie. Esther let the ringing go on. She needed to finish her homework before returning to school if she was going to maintain her trajectory toward valedictorian. Sophie was hot on her heels for first place.

A text. *Hey.* It was from Sophie.

Esther picked Molly up and put her in her lap. Her cell phone chimed, telling her she had another text. *Come to the window.*

A smile tipped the corner of Esther's mouth. She closed her laptop, took off her glasses, put Molly on the floor, and leaned out the open window. She could see Sophie's white T-shirt against the ivy on the trellis she was climbing. Her jet-black hair was up in a tight ponytail, like Esther's. They called it the geek-girl look.

"Esther!" With raised eyebrows, Sophie half whispered and half growled, looking up at the window shaking her head.

"Oh crepes! I can't believe I forgot." Esther moved the laptop, lay across her desk, and put her hands out to pull Sophie over the window frame and into the room. She turned her lamp on, and Sophie brushed dirt off her shirt. "I am so sorry, Sophie. I can't go."

"What? You've got to go! I snuck out!"

"I just . . . "

"I don't care who died! There will never be another moment like this. You pinky swore. You can't miss a chance to see the author of *Blessed Be*. I read her book in one night. It's about witches who live in a town just like this one"

Esther sighed. "I heard Madison Merriweather was a witch herself and writes about what she knows best."

"Who cares? Her books are great. She's one witch I want to meet." Sophie glanced nervously at the door to Esther's bedroom

"Don't worry. They're still gone on their honeymoon."

"Good. I don't want that man arresting me."

Esther laughed. "He won't. He's cool . . . so far. Anyway, Mary is sleeping with Grandma Mable in the apartment around back while they're gone, and Hope is in Mary's room, across the hall. She won't tell."

"Does she want to go? Did you ask her? I mean, who wouldn't want to go?" Sophie asked as she moved to the door.

"Sophie!" Esther whispered. Sophie was through the door before she could stop her. She went out into the hall.

Across the hall, the door was open, and the light was still on in seventeen-year-old Hope's room. She was sitting cross-legged on her bed with math homework spread out around her. Her red curls were in a messy bun, and three pencils were stuck in it. She was rubbing her forehead and chewing on the eraser of another pencil. The family's old dog, a cocker spaniel named Lady, had her head in her lap.

"Hey, Hope," Sophie said, as if showing up around eleven o'clock on a school night was nothing new.

"Hey, Sophie," Hope replied. Esther couldn't believe it. Hope didn't even look up. True, she had been homeless, and her life had been kind of rough before coming to live with Esther's family last month, but seriously, it was eleven on a school night. Wasn't Hope curious?

Apparently the time of night didn't slow Sophie down. "Did you hear about the midnight book launch and signing at Seaside Stories? We're going witch hunting. Want to come?"

"Huh?" Hope looked confused.

"Sophie, I shouldn't go," Esther said.

"You're coming. Come on! How often does a world-famous author come to a town like Necanicum? Come on, my . . . "

"Don't say it!" Esther pointed at Sophie's face.

"Witches! I was going to say, 'Come on, my witches!' You are such a goody-goody, Esther." Sophie laughed. "Get your hoodie. Come on!"

"I'm in." Hope piled her math homework onto the floor, gently helped the old dog move, and then stood up and stretched.

"Shouldn't we tell Grandma Mable?" Esther asked.

Hope checked her cell phone. "Nah, it's eleven. She'll call if she's worried."

"Now I know you've had too much freedom."

Hope smiled. "I was just downstairs. The door to her room was closed last time I looked. She's asleep, and Mary is sleeping on the couch in Mable's room. No reason to wake them."

"Come on!" Sophie pushed Esther to the door of the bedroom and across the hall to her own room. She took a white Oceanside High sweatshirt off the hook by the door, handed it to Esther, and waited while she put it on. Hope joined them, and then Sophie climbed onto the desk to go back out the window.

Hope turned around and said, "Later, witches. I'm taking the stairs."

Esther laughed at Sophie, who did a face palm and joined her, following Hope through the dark house to the front door. They both stopped when the long wooden stairs in the old Victorian creaked. Nothing. No one moved.

They picked their way across the dark living room and out the heavy oak door that squeaked when it opened. Once they crossed the large front porch and made it to the sidewalk, Hope was the first to break the silence.

"So, who's the big deal author coming to Seaside Stories?"

Sophie looked at her with large brown eyes. "You seriously don't know? Where have you been?"

Hope turned to Sophie, with her eyebrows raised. "Orphaned, homeless, in foster care, fishing." She shrugged and laughed.

"Oh, yeah." Sophie looked embarrassed, but they all giggled together quietly in the night air. True, it sounded bizarre, but it had become sort of a fact of life. After all, what else could Hope do when life was this bizarre? Laugh, because if she told someone what really happened, they'd think she'd made it up.

Hope had been homeless before Mable had taken her in and become her foster mom. As usual, Esther was on the outside and didn't know too many details. The more chaotic life got, the more Esther focused on school.

They walked toward the ocean and then turned onto the sidewalk that ran the distance of the seawall into town. To the west, the ocean rolled in and out on the sandy beach. To the east, Esther's house was just beyond the trees. It blended into a mishmash of old and new, large and small homes that climbed the wooded mountain.

Old-fashioned street lamps made the seawall welcoming in the night. Couples held hands and walked, a boy on a skateboard held onto the seat of his buddy's bike, letting the bike rider pull him down the sidewalk, and an old man in the distance picked up the poop his dog dropped, telling his Lab he was a good boy.

The girls walked, and Sophie explained to Hope what was happening. "Madison Merriweather, the author of *Blessed Be*, is here. You know, *Blessed Be*? The book with the witch's hat on the front? The one everyone is reading?" Sophie walked backwards facing Hope and Esther, gesturing wildly as she tried to make Hope understand.

"I haven't had much time for reading." Hope smiled.

"I can't believe you haven't heard of her! She lives in Seattle, with her two cats, Salem and Lucifer. She says she isn't a witch and none of it is real, but everyone wants to live in the black castle in the book."

"So, what's happening tonight?" Hope asked.

Esther chimed in. "Well, I guess Madison Merriweather's childhood best friend just moved to Necanicum. No one knows who it is, but Madison is releasing her second book tonight, revealing her best friend, and saying she has some big announcement."

"Don't you see?" Sophie asked. "This is huge! I heard a celebrity is in town and will introduce her and everything. What if, like, you know—she's giving something away? What if she makes a movie and we get a job as extras?"

"I don't have enough to buy her book," Esther said.

"I can buy it for you," Hope said. "I've got some tip money with me from the coffee shop." She rattled the pocket of her hoodie.

"Her books are like, thirty dollars," Sophie said. "I've only got enough cash because I haven't eaten lunch ever since I heard she was coming to town."

"Won't your mom buy it for you?" Hope asked Sophie.

"Nah. She thinks it's a devil book. We're churchgoers, you know? Our pastor says we shouldn't read books that talk about things like witches. What about your church, Esther?"

Esther shrugged. What the church thought hadn't crossed her mind. "With everything that's been happening, I haven't thought about it."

"I've been meaning to ask," Sophie said. "Is there any update on how your dad is doing?"

"No, he's still healing and will be returned to the regular prison cells when the doctors release him." Esther's mind drifted. She was walking with the girls, but she was far away, remembering. She could see Mom telling her the news. Her father had escaped from prison. He might try to find them . . .

Sophie interrupted her thoughts. "Did you decide? Are you going to write to him?"

Esther was silent.

"Hey. Let's just have fun, okay?" Hope said and gave Sophie a glaring look as she gave Esther's shoulders a side hug.

"Oh, right. Sorry." Sophie was suddenly silent.

"Whoa!" Hope said, bringing Esther back to the present. There were hundreds of people downtown. They could see them a few blocks away, in the distance surrounding the bookstore.

"How are we ever going to get in? We should have camped out this afternoon." Sophie looked deflated.

"Hey, wait, look!" Esther couldn't believe her eyes. In the middle of the mass of people she saw Nephi, a head and shoulders taller than most men, with sun-streaked brown hair like hers.

He was talking to a reporter from the local paper. Roger Abbott was a gray-haired, lean man, who always wore a fedora. He was holding out a small microphone to Nephi, who was saying something Esther couldn't make out in the chaos.

"Come on!" Hope said above the noise of the crowd and took Sophie's and Esther's hands. They pushed through the crowd toward Nephi.

"Wait!" Esther said. "Aren't we going to get into trouble if he tells on us?"

Hope shook her head and gave a loud laugh. "How can he tell on us? He's here."

After several minutes of pushing past people who were none too happy to lose their place in the crowd, the girls made it to Nephi.

"Nephi!" Sophie called. He gave her a confused look.

*That's Nephi. Always joking around.*

His face broke into a smile.

"You guys are in trouble." He pointed at them and laughed hard.

"If we are, then so are you," Hope said, green eyes twinkling.

Nephi threw his head back and let out a loud chuckle. For a big guy, he had an infectious laugh. Then he stepped aside and nudged someone forward.

"Do you guys know Parker?" Nephi asked.

Esther's pulse quickened, and her stomach dropped. There he was, the beautiful Parker Stuart, and there right beside him was his twin, Paisley. *Ugh.* She went by all three-names—Paisley Pamela Stuart—on social media, and there she was taking a selfie with duck lips, while Esther stared.

Roger Abbott was also staring at Paisley. She had dressed her five-foot-eleven frame in all black, with a tight blonde ponytail and hot pink lips, and was making faces into her cell phone. She was with a girl who dressed and acted like Paisley, except with black hair—the dark to Paisley's light.

To make matters worse, she and Parker had just moved to Necanicum from England and talked with an English accent. *Chez adorbs* was an understatement. Everyone in school was totally infatuated with their accents, including Esther.

Nephi slapped Parker on the back, pushing him toward the girls. Parker bumped Paisley, who scowled at him.

Parker looked at Esther and then at the ground, with his hands in his pockets. His ponytail matched Paisley's perfectly, and Esther wondered if they'd planned it. But his black T-shirt stretched across his muscular shoulders looked much different from Paisley's.

"Hello, ladies," Parker said.

Even his short greeting sounded cute with his accent.

Before anyone could reply, Roger Abbott pushed Parker aside, put the little microphone in Esther's face, and began speaking rapidly.

"Esther, how do you feel about your father's recent escape from prison? Is it true he came to your house to kidnap you last month and tried to traffic kids on the coast?" Abbott asked.

Eyes wide, Esther froze. Somewhere in the middle of his speech, she stopped hearing Abbott. The sound of rushed water in her ears and blood pumped so hard and fast it was all she could hear. Time stood still, like a slow-motion scene from a horror movie.

"Knock it off, man! What's wrong with you?" Parker asked.

Esther turned. Parker had come to her rescue. He had pulled himself up to his full height, with his hands out of his pockets and balled into fists.

Nephi, always the voice of reason, chimed in. "Listen, Abbott. That was vicious. Totally uncalled for. Our moms aren't even here."

Abbot looked up, way up, at Nephi's calm face and over to Parker's angry stare. "Yeah, it's a party. Not the time. Sorry, Esther. I'll call your mom." Abbot pushed a short bald man out of his way and blended into the crowd. Paisley walked with her friend toward the bookstore.

Still surprised by Parker coming to the rescue, Esther said quietly, "Thanks, Parker."

He nodded.

"You're awesome!" Sophie exclaimed. She put her hand up and waited for Parker to high-five her. Parker's face broke into a crooked grin, and he gave her a limp high-five, which was more like a depressed four-and-a-half.

"So what brings you nerds out past bedtime?" Nephi asked.

"Hey!" Hope exclaimed.

"I was talking about the girl geek squad." Nephi pointed at Esther and Sophie.

"Geeks rule," Sophie said. "Nerds are the best, man. Someday we'll rule the world and you'll be begging for a job as our janitor!"

Esther cringed. She knew Nephi was embarrassed about his low-to-average grades. But Sophie wouldn't stop. "What brings you out?" Struggling for a comeback, she added, "You . . . athlete."

Parker laughed out loud, and it sounded just as wonderful as his accent.

"He came with me. I made him," Parker said. "My mum's friend is launching a book and . . . "

"Shut the front door!" Sophie looked as if someone had just told her she had won the lottery. "Wait! Wait!"

"You're repeating yourself," Nephi said.

"Wait. Wait. Madison Merriweather is your mom's friend? Are you kidding me? You know her? I . . . I . . . " Sophie was at a loss for words. Esther had never seen Sophie at a loss for words. She could talk anyone under the table.

"That's what he said." Hope took Sophie by her short shoulders and turned her around to face her. "Calm down, fangirl."

Esther looked at Parker, who was grinning and laughing. "Sorry."

"No. Don't apologize. Madison loves her fans. Do you want to meet her?" Parker asked.

"Are you kidding? Are you kidding me?" Sophie jumped up and down and began fanning herself like a beauty queen getting a crown.

"Come on," Parker said, gesturing for them to follow him. As he pushed through the crowd and into the bookstore, he put his arm around Esther's shoulders and pulled her along. She let him direct her while her heart beat faster and faster. "Excuse me. Pardon me." He kept smiling, and people smiled right back and were happy to let him into the store ahead of them.

*Wow, who is this guy? He is so nice. Popular and nice,* Esther thought as he took his arm off and reached for the doors to the bookstore.

"Are you okay?" Hope asked Esther.

"No," she said.

"You don't have to be, you know."

"Thanks." Esther gave Hope a lame smile.

Once they passed through the large vintage double doors, a wall of heat hit her. After the chill of the evening air, it felt suffocating. The outside crowd of people who had made it into the store were massed shoulder to shoulder, chatting, looking at books, and waiting for the author.

They kept pushing toward the grand staircase that was behind an island with the cash register in the center of the store. The wide stairway wound from the center main floor to a second-floor loft, where they kept the leather-bound antiques in heavy oak bookcases. They'd chained it off for the evening.

Jack, the young bookstore owner, was wearing his traditional argyle sweater and reading glasses on a gold chain. He looked stuffy to Esther. He was behind the register with Hazel, his oldest employee. Hazel had come with the store when Jack had bought it.

"Everybody line up!" Hazel called in her Southern drawl. She would never be a local because she used words like *y'all.* "Bless your hearts. I know you're excited, but we must maintain order." Hazel's short gray hair, which was usually well ordered, looked as chaotic as the night.

At the base of the stairs, next to a table with a stack of *Blessed Be* books, was a thick woman wearing a black pants suit. She was dripping in diamonds. Her hair was large, curly, and just plain impressive. But her eyelashes were definitely pasted on under glittering green eye shadow. Her nails matched her eye shadow, and so did the stones in the layers of bracelets she wore. She tossed back her head and gave a catty laugh at something a thin, beautiful blonde said. The blonde was an older version of Paisley.

"Hi, Mum," Parker said to the blonde. She smiled and gave him a hug.

Parker pointed at Sophie. "This is my friend . . . " The look on his face let Esther know he was drawing a total blank on Sophie's name.

"Sophie," she said, putting her hand out to the author and bouncing on her toes. "And this is my best friend, Esther, and her new sister, Hope. We're humongous fans!" Finally, she had to take a breath. "Wait! Let me take a selfie." Sophie pulled out her phone, leaned closer to Madison, and made duck lips while she snapped several shots. "Esther, Parker, get in here."

Mortified, Esther looked at the author while she and Parker got closer, leaning into the shot. Being so close to Parker made her uncomfortable and tingly all at the same time. Parker, she noticed, smiled brilliantly and posed comfortably.

The author looked down her nose at Sophie, one eyebrow raised, and her mouth pursed as if she'd eaten a lemon slice. "Thank you. Tag me in your post. Would you like me to sign a book for you?"

"Yes, oh yes, please!" Sophie picked up two books and took another selfie of her face and the book covers. She thrust an open book toward the author. "I want both of your books signed. Can you write, *To my friend, Sophie?*"

Madison Merriweather didn't miss a beat. "To my friend . . . how do I spell Sophie?"

While the author signed the book, Esther, though embarrassed, was loving Sophie's exuberance. Esther stole a glance at Parker and caught him looking at her. "I'm sorry."

"You say that a lot," he said.

"Sorry." It came out of her mouth before she could stop herself.

He laughed. "You have got to stop that. You have nothing to be sorry for."

*If only he knew.*

He leaned toward her and said, "Nephi told me what happened with your dad. Now it's my turn to be sorry. I hate it when parents fight, or worse."

Suddenly, her embarrassment was over. "It's not like that. My mom is the best. It isn't her fault." *It's mine.*

"I didn't mean to say it was your mum's fault. It's just, there's always two sides to the story."

Now she was furious. "No there isn't. Sometimes people are just awful, and they do terrible things, and no one is to blame but them!" And then she had the thought that always followed any conversation about her parents. *It's all my fault.*

Hope stepped between her and Parker. Esther wasn't seeing Hope. She was seeing red. She was someplace far away, standing behind the couch, and small, too small to see over it.

"Sophie, are you done?" Hope asked over the buzz of the bookstore crowd. "It's time to go home." She gently took Sophie by the elbow and started leading her to the door.

"Wait! I want to hear the announcement, and I have to pay for my books," Sophie said.

"Hurry up!" Hope told her.

Esther followed Hope and waited by the door with her, watching Sophie get in line behind a half-dozen people waiting to pay for their books.

Paisley passed Parker with the girl who looked like her evil twin. She looked like Paisley, except her hair was black and her eyes were dark—not just brown—but dark as if they sucked the light right out of the room. Obviously Parker's friend too, the girl was looking at Parker and Nephi as if they were fresh meat. Then she pulled out her cell and began snapping selfies with Paisley.

"Who's that?" Esther asked. Hope shrugged and started texting.

A short bald man in a wrinkled gray suit photo bombed Paisley's selfie and then waved at her.

"Paisley! It's me!" He smiled.

Paisley looked over her shoulder to see who was calling her. When she spotted him, her eyes grew large, and she laughed. Her friend leaned in to her, and they cackled.

The man's head dropped, a dark look passing over his face as he slunk away. He sent a shiver down Esther's spine.

"Can I have your attention, please?" Jack, the bookstore owner, shouted over the din. "Attention, everyone. I would like to introduce our newest Necanicum resident, Melissa Hearst-Stuart."

Jack pointed at Parker's mother, who stood on the stairs, to be seen above the crowd and cleared his throat. "I am thrilled to introduce my lifetime bestie. The best-selling author of *Blessed Be*, Madison Merriweather!"

The crowd clapped wildly.

"Thank you." Madison pointed back at Parker's mom. "Melissa Hearst-Stuart, people. Can a girl get a better best friend?" She gave a golf clap, and the room joined her while Melissa posed. "I am proud to officially launch my new book in your quaint town." Madison held up a black book with a silver snowflake embossed on the front. "*Winter Solstice*, a young adult fantasy and the second book in my series."

Hope was texting someone frantically. Esther leaned back against the cool wall and wished she could sink into it. She couldn't believe she yelled at Parker after he'd just saved her. *I'm such an idiot. Maybe I should go say I'm sorry, one hundred more times.*

The author went on. "And I am pleased to introduce M. Slade Baxter, the director of the movie *Blessed Be*, to be filmed in Necanicum, Oregon."

The room exploded. People cheered, whistled, and clapped. Sophie screamed so loud Esther had to smile. Sophie jumped up and down and only stopped to push her way closer to the mic and take another selfie. Several cell phones raised above the crowd and flashed photos of the moment. Esther took hers out of her pocket and took a quick pic of the event.

"We will use extras from town!"

"Me! Me! Me!" Sophie squealed, raising one hand like she was in class. The crowd laughed and applauded Madison's news.

Roger Abbott was filming the announcement, but he was quickly shut out by big city reporters from a Portland news stations. They were gathered around the author, asking questions.

Esther searched for Parker. He stood quietly by his mother, scanning the room. Then his eyes met hers. She quickly looked down. When she looked back up, he was still staring.

"Hope, let's go."

"Where's Sophie?" Hope asked.

"In that long line."

"We shouldn't leave her behind." Hope stopped texting and looked at Esther. "I'm sure you're sick of people asking, but are you going to be all right until we get home? I know it isn't easy in a small town. Trust me. Give it time. It's only been a month or so since it happened. The whole town knows why I was put in foster care and live with Mable. I understand what it's like to be a victim of small-town gossip. Sometimes I feel guilty for having complicated your family's life by moving in with your grandma."

"Hope. Don't be silly. Your mom died. You needed us, and we love you. It's just, he's my father. Everyone knows my dad did really bad things and tried to kidnap me. I feel like my life is a crappy novel. No one will ever treat me the same."

"At least we're in it together." Hope gave her a quick hug. Esther hugged her back. They both looked at the cash register for Sophie, standing side by side, trying not to notice Parker and Nephi staring at them and talking to each other.

"They're talking about us," Esther said.

"I know. Here comes Sophie."

Grinning like a little kid who had just been told they had the run of a candy store, she made her way toward them with both books held high and waving. They gave her a wan smile and, as soon as she was close enough, walked her outside.

The cold night air was bracing. People from the crowd pushed into the store, filling the spaces they left behind. Across the street, a large black truck was idling, with a vinyl fish decal on the side. The driver's tinted window rolled down and revealed Fisher, Hope's boyfriend. He gave them a silly grin, a man nod, and wave. Hope quickly went to Fisher's door, stepped on the stainless running board, and gave him a kiss on the cheek.

"Thanks for the pickup, babe," Hope said.

"Oh! Aren't they adorable?" Sophie held her books, as if they were precious cargo, right to her chest and went to the passenger's side.

Hope opened the passenger door, climbed up into the lifted truck, and gave Sophie a hand up. Esther and Hope squeezed together into the large leather seat. Sophie sat on their laps and forced the door shut.

"Thanks, Fisher," Esther said.

"No problem. Hope told me about Abbott. Jerk. I heard the new kid, Parker, gave him a lesson in manners. Where's Nephi? Does he need a ride too?"

"No!" Esther was still embarrassed and not ready to face Parker.

Fisher gave her a suspicious look and pulled away from the curb.

"Hey! Wait!" Nephi and Parker came sprinting out of the crowd. Fisher stopped the truck. Using the rear bumper, they climbed into the back.

Fisher opened the slider window in the cab and asked the boys, "Where to?"

"The cove," Nephi said.

Sophie waved and smiled at Nephi and Parker.

"Of course, the cove," Esther said to Sophie once the window was closed again.

"Yeah, he's a rich boy," Sophie said. "He's hot, and he likes you. You gotta stop moping around. You didn't even say hello."

"Hey," Hope interrupted. "Give her some time."

Pulling out her phone, Sophie smiled at Esther and began swiping through her photos. "Darn. There's a weird man photo bombing some of my best shots. Look how cute you are with Parker." She held up the phone for Esther to see.

"Did it ruin your picture with the author?" Esther saw the short man in the picture. He was looking at Paisley. Sophie showed her the next picture, and he was in the shot looking at Sophie or the author.

Hope looked at the photo and shook her head. "It'll get better, Esther. Promise."

Esther looked at Hope.

Hope, whose mother had died only a few months ago.

Hope, in foster care with Esther's family and still trying to make her feel better.

A little tear escaped her eye and ran down her face. But this time it wasn't because she was sad. It was because she felt so much love for Hope, strong Hope.

# 4

# Blood Is Thicker than Water

The alarm went off, making Molly meow and stretch. She had been sleeping on Esther's hair. Esther rolled onto her back, and Molly climbed onto her stomach and continued stretching and kneading the blanket with her claws.

"I don't want to get up either, Miss Molly. But I have to go back to school," Esther said. Molly licked her paws; then she lay across Esther's neck and purred.

"No, you don't." Esther gently pulled her off and looked in her blue eyes. "We will get extra credit and beat out Sophie, somehow."

She made her bed before she pulled on her ironed jeans, a pressed cotton button-up white blouse, and a navy-blue nerd sweater. Or, at least, that's what Nephi called it. After removing any traces of Molly's fur with a roller, she brushed out her hair.

She had been about to put her hair up into a complicated side sweeping fishtail braid when she opened Facebook to check for messages and saw the post.

The large font in the social media post read, "Family Crisis Center Advocate's Ex-husband Arrested for Attempted Kidnapping After Escaping Prison Work Release Program, by Roger Abbott." It was from the local newspaper's page. It didn't say a thing about how after it was all over, he had asked her mother for forgiveness. *I want to hate him, but he's my dad. He wasn't mean all the time. He's never asked for forgiveness before. What if he changes?*

Esther threw her phone onto the bed.

"Everyone knows," she said to Molly. Her heart was beating so fast, she could feel it trying to break. She put her hand on her chest and sat down hard on the edge of her bed. Molly jumped onto the bed and rubbed against her back. Scooping her up and holding her, Esther's thoughts wandered through the puzzle. How did Abbott know so much?

Abbot's post must have turned up on her feed because someone tagged her in a comment. She picked the phone up with her free hand and scrolled through the comments. They sent her over the edge, from feeling anxious to a sensation of being doomed. People's comments ranged from feeling sorry for her family to sizzling hatred. Everything from "Grace is the domestic violence advocate that helped my wife leave me. Now look who needs help. She should be fired," to tiny emoji hands praying for them. She couldn't stop reading. It was like seeing an oncoming train and being so fascinated she forgot to step out of the way.

Abbott had posted a mugshot from her father's original arrest when he was finally found and taken to jail for trying to kill her mother—the reason they had moved three states to hide in Coho County.

The article said, "Domestic/sexual assault advocate who's supposed to support survivors has her own mess to clean up."

Triggered, and unable to stop her racing thoughts, a childhood memory played itself out like a B movie reel in her mind. She was little, hiding. How old was she? Eight, almost nine? But she could smell the memory, feel it as if it were happening today.

She'd been crying. She didn't remember why, but it was the last time she'd ever wailed out loud. She learned her lesson. Her tantrum had started the fight. *Be quiet. Stop crying. He can't handle it. My fault. Stop . . .*

"Run," Esther said out loud to her empty room. But her mother hadn't run. She'd almost died.

Molly meowed in confusion and batted at Esther's face. Esther shook her head, took a deep breath, and willed herself back into the present.

She curled up in her bed, her body wrapped around her cat, holding her, closing her eyes and feeling tears run down her cheeks.

Her cell phone rang. Sophie was sending her more pictures and selfies from the book signing. She knew she should answer it, but she just wanted the world to go away. They had moved to the coast to hide, and now everything was ruined. Images of her mother's sad face when she saw the news paralyzed her. When the ringtone finally stopped, she could hear the ocean. She loved this place and didn't want to leave.

*I can't do this.* She pulled the covers over her head. She didn't hear her Grandma Mable call to her from downstairs, saying goodbye when she left for work. She didn't hear Nephi drive away in his old truck. She was far away, hiding behind the leather couch.

Hours passed. Esther had gotten up only once to go to the bathroom and to feed Miss Molly. She lay down and put a cold washcloth on her face. She was under the covers trying to will the world away when she heard Sophie calling for her.

"Esther!" A tiny pebble came through Esther's open window and then another. They bounced on the hardwood floor of the old house.

Esther hung her head out of the second-story window. A rock hit her in the forehead. "Ouch!"

"Sorry," Sophie said and then disappeared from view. Esther heard her open the front door. Sophie's feet stomped up the stairs. She sat on one side of Esther's bed.

"What's wrong with you?" Sophie asked, going on without waiting for an answer. "Why are you not in school? I had to do library sciences all by myself. Do I need to call your mom? Are you sick?"

"Did you see what the newspaper posted online?" she asked, holding out her phone.

"Yeah, so?" Sophie walked over and took Esther's phone, typed in Esther's pin, and scrolled with her thumb. "They're idiots. What do you care?"

"Did you read the comments?" She put her hands out, and Molly came to her, letting Esther pick her up and pet her.

"Are you kidding? I was reading my new book all night. Let me see." Sophie scrolled back and clicked on something. Her eyebrows drew together as she mouthed the words. Then, in horror, she looked up at Esther, silent for what seemed to be forever.

"You gotta ignore this stuff. It's garbage! You need to get out of bed. It's lunchtime and we have to get back before classes start. You can still make it to gym class."

Esther nodded and stood, putting Molly down.

"Comb your hair. Do you want Parker to see you looking like that?"

"What does he care?"

"He's been asking about you all morning. He feels really bad," Sophie said while handing her a hairbrush.

"Did he say that?" Esther asked.

"For being so smart, you sure are dumb. He didn't have to. Crepes! He asked me three times where you were. You know. In that accent." She made a serious face. "'Ello. 'Ave you seen Est-tar?"

"Really?"

"Move! We can't be late to gym class. We won't get an A." Sophie pushed her toward the bedroom door. Molly followed them through the house until they gently pushed her back inside and closed the front door.

The darkness in her heart lifted, a little smile rising in the morning sun. They trotted toward school, chatting in an English accent.

# 5

# "A" for Effort

Esther and Sophie ran through the double doors into an empty gymnasium.

"Where is everyone?" Esther asked.

"We must have missed the bus! Today is bowling. We are in so much trouble. We can't get an A if we miss two classes, and this is my second miss."

"Mine too."

"Do you think we could run to the bowling alley and he might forgive us for being late?" Sophie asked.

"It's worth a try. How far is it?"

"It can't be more than a mile."

"I'm game," Esther said.

They turned and rushed out the door. Both girls still had on their backpacks. They ran along the side of Highway 101. It didn't have sidewalks, so they had to run single file until they reached the bridge that crossed the river leading to the harbor.

"This is taking too long," Sophie said as they trotted side by side over the bridge.

"Don't give up."

Picking up their pace, they sprinted the last half mile. They hit the doors to the bowling alley at full speed and only came to a stop when they were standing in front of Coach Johansson at the bowling shoe counter. Both girls were panting hard.

"How did you girls get here?" the short, round coach asked.

"We . . . ran," Esther said. "We don't want to lose our grades."

Coach Johansson pushed up the baseball cap he was wearing and scratched his bald forehead. Still silent, he scratched his gray beard, thinking. The girls waited anxiously. He straightened out his whistle on its lanyard.

"Well?" Sophie asked.

"Well . . . " Coach Johansson said. "I can't give you credit for showing up late today, but you girls will need some extra credit to bring your grades up to the A you want. I'll tell you what, come to my office after school and bring tennis shoes."

When the final bell rang, Esther and Sophie met outside the coach's office door.

"I wonder what we need our tennis shoes for," Esther said.

"He'll probably make us run laps."

"I wouldn't mind. I like running, sort of."

"That's because your legs aren't two feet long," Sophie said.

Esther laughed. "Too true."

The coach came down the hall, carrying his bowling bag. They waited while he unlocked his office door and followed him in. He opened a cabinet and put the bag on the bottom shelf and turned to look at the girls, with a sly grin on his face.

"I am so glad you came voluntarily to get some extra credit."

"Not exactly vol—" Sophie started to say, but the coach interrupted her.

"As you know, track season is upon us, and the long distance track team is running. As you may not know, I do not have enough girls participating in long distance track this year. In fact, there is only one girl on the team. It makes me look bad," Coach Johansson said.

"We've never done track. It takes too much time away from math and science," Esther said.

"I know you both want to go to college, and I'm betting you're already applying for scholarships. Perhaps, you've noticed that having a sport makes your college applications more attractive. I will do you a favor and you will make my numbers look good until the end of the school year. Then if you want to quit, you can."

Esther couldn't believe it. She felt as if she were being blackmailed.

"So all we have to do is show up to long distance track, right?" Sophie asked.

"That's right. I'm hoping you'll enjoy it and stay, but if you drop out in the summer, I'll understand," the coach said.

"So, who's the other girl?" Esther asked.

"Paisley Stuart," the coach said. "You can start today, or I'm willing to be really generous and let you get some running clothes and come back tomorrow."

"Okay. See you tomorrow." Esther couldn't wait to get out of his office. Nephi wasn't on the only one on the team. Parker was on the team with Nephi, and this meant she had to wear shorts, sweat, and run in front of Parker.

# 6

# Run for Cover

Sweat poured down Esther's face as she tried to keep up with Sophie, Nephi, and Parker. Never mind Paisley, who had sprinted ahead, looking like a sweat-free sportswear model.

"I can't believe how good I am at running." Sophie grinned at Esther. She was almost as fast as Nephi on her short little legs. She ran with ease around the boys, talking and flitting from one to the other like a bumblebee. Only Esther seemed to struggle.

They ran on the sidewalk to avoid traffic and headed toward the beach. Most drivers swung wide when the runners crossed the streets or if there wasn't any sidewalk, but a green sedan slowed down and paced Esther. She refused to make eye contact or even look at the driver. The last thing she wanted was to be seen by anyone in town in her black baggy running shorts.

Nephi looked over his shoulder and called back to her, "Come on, Esther. You got this!"

The team left the road and ran down the beach access onto the soft white sand, where every step took ten times the effort.

She rolled her eyes and shook her head at Nephi. *I got this all right. I got a heart attack with a side of sweat.*

Parker let Nephi go ahead and slowed his pace, jogging along easily. His muscular arms and legs pumped effortlessly, and he looked like a professional football player just trotting off the field. *It's like watching a work of art. No—ballet? Is he even sweating?*

Parker's head turned, and she realized, in horror, that he would see her like this. She looked away and did anything she could to keep their eyes from meeting. *No! No. What is he doing?* Parker slowed his gait even more and fell back to run alongside Esther.

Esther tried to open her mouth more, to make space in her airways and end the huffing and puffing sounds she was making, but still wouldn't look at him.

Parker broke the silence. "I remember when I first started. I could hardly breathe. Just crossing the soft sand was a killer."

Somehow she doubted anything was hard for him. Although it was easier now that they were running closer to the water on the dark, hard sand, all she wanted to do was stop running and die. Esther looked up. They were going toward the cove where the beach ended in rocks and a mountain.

"How far?" she asked.

"Just to the trailhead and back. Past the cove parking lot and a mile up the mountain to the trail parking lot. You know?" Parker pointed to the midway point on the mountain.

Esther stopped dead in her tracks, bent over, and put her hands on her knees, gasping for air. She straightened. He was slowly jogging circles around her.

"You're doing great," he said and smiled sheepishly at her.

She took one more deep breath and started running again. It wasn't long until they arrived at the rocks. They varied in size from small to two or three-foot boulders piled up, requiring beachgoers to climb them to get to the parking lot.

People regularly tried to make trails through the rocks, but the powerful ocean would just rise and rearrange the stones and boulders a few weeks later.

They both had to go slower. The rocks closer to the water were slick with seaweed. Walking and hopping from rock to rock, she was careful not to slip or twist an ankle. Her lungs were on fire.

Parker was ahead of her and on top of a larger boulder. He reached back and took her hand, helping her balance until she made it to the next small rock.

"My mum's friend is filming and holding a party at our house," he said. "Do you think Sophie would like to check it out?"

"Duh," was all she could get out. She was still out of breath.

When they arrived at the parking lot, they began slowly jogging up the road to the mountain trail, trying to catch up to Nephi and Sophie, who were a good half mile ahead of them. Paisley was nowhere to be found.

The green sedan passed them, going back to town. The driver was the bald man who'd waved at Paisley from the bookstore. He looked at Esther and quickly turned his head away.

She stopped. "Did he have on pink lipstick?" she asked Parker.

"What?" He looked back at the car, which was well down the road. "I missed it. Anyway, they're going to be making a movie at our house."

"Your house? You mean your mansion. What time are they filming?" Esther asked.

"Well, I don't know if they're actually filming, but the stars are meeting for dinner Friday night and going to see the house."

"Stars? Who's in the movie?"

"No idea. Madeline won't tell us. We just have to be ready for about ten dinner guests at seven," he said. "I can't invite you to dinner, but we're close to my house. Let's run one more block and I'll show you where you could hide and watch." He gave her a mischievous grin.

"Will the castle dogs chase us?"

"Ha ha. Very funny. No, but General Cornwallis may take you prisoner."

"I thought Cornwallis surrendered in Yorktown?" she said, laughing.

He chuckled. "Cornwallis is our Labradoodle."

"The real general has been demoted to an allergy-free doodle? Poor Cornwallis. My cat is named after a historical figure too."

"See, I knew we had something in common. What's your cat's name?"

"Molly Brown, after the unsinkable Molly Brown, survivor of the *Titanic*."

"Oh, but she was so much more than unsinkable. She went back to look for survivors. Could your cat do that? Parker asked.

"Um, no. That's a definite no. She isn't that fond of water. She would let us drown." Esther laughed.

"There's our house." He nodded toward a four-story Queen Anne-style house, a mansion to Esther. Everyone knew his father, the new hospital chief executive officer, had purchased the historic Captain's Cove Mansion. It was on all the local tourist maps as having belonged to a sea captain who built it in the late eighteen hundreds, complete with a widow's walk. High among the gables, a square tower had windows on every side. Esther was sure you could see the ocean from every window.

The house had a wrought-iron gate, with an ornate iron fence running across the front and into the woods behind it. It was pointed and would have been fierce looking if it hadn't been waist high.

"Why is the fence so low?" she asked.

"I expect so it doesn't interfere with the view," he answered. "Follow me."

He took a small trail that ran along the outside of the fence on the left side of the house and deep into the woods. They had only gone a few feet past his home when she got a look at the backyard. It had a vintage white gazebo in the center, large enough for two long dinner tables set end to end. Twinkle lights were being hung by a local handyman. The fence ended, and a creek cut through the property. The green lawns, the large old-growth pines, and the white lights made it picture perfect.

"Over here." He motioned to her, and she followed.

High up in what looked like an ancient oak tree competing for light among the pines was a spacious tree house. It was balanced in the arms of the branches, with odd-shaped pieces of wood nailed to the trunk. He climbed it, pushed open a trapdoor, and disappeared inside. She followed. The little tree house looked like it hadn't been used in a while, but it had a window with a beautiful view of the backyard.

"We found this when we bought the house," he explained. "See how close you are to the gazebo where we'll serve dinner? You and Sophie should be able to hear almost every word, and if you can't, just text me. I will have them speak up for you." He chuckled at his joke.

"Won't someone see us out here?"

"Not if you're careful," he said and began climbing down. "If I don't have to be at dinner, I'll sneak out to see you. In fact, I promise you both a surprise."

"No surprises, all right?" She laughed nervously. "My mother would kill me if she knew. How am I going to get out past Grandma?"

"You snuck out for the book signing. You'll figure it out. I hear it's the American way." Parker gave her a crooked grin.

Her knees went weak. *He's trouble.*

"We'd better catch up to the others." Esther's voice shook, and she almost ran for the trapdoor. As she rushed to climb down the wood pieces nailed to the tree, her shoe slipped and she lost her footing, so she jumped the five feet to reach the ground, where she landed sideways on the moist ground. Her right leg and hip were smeared with mud.

"Are you okay?" Parker held out his hand to help her up. She put her muddy right hand in his, and he easily lifted her to her feet.

"Fantastic." Gingerly she took a few steps and tested her legs. "No harm done. Go ahead. I'll catch up."

"Promise?"

"Go!"

"Okay. I guess I should pick up my pace so coach is happy." Parker grinned as he waved goodbye, leaving her behind and sprinting up the mountain.

"Help," Esther said to herself. She took a deep breath and followed him. Sophie and Nephi passed her going the other way, already heading back to the school.

"Sophie!" Esther turned around, cut her run short, and raced after Sophie to give her the news.

# 7

# In the Driver's Seat

"Why does he have to come?" Sophie whined.

"Maybe because I have the truck," Nephi retorted.

"Move over." Sophie squeezed into Nephi's little truck. "What kind of truck is this?"

"A Ford. I'm a Ford man."

"I didn't know Ford made dented red trucks." Sophie ran her finger along a crack in the window.

"Hey," Nephi said, frowning. "It's a classic."

Esther snickered.

"Laugh it up, nerd. You want me to keep quiet, right? We both know your mom wouldn't approve of you two alone in a tree house with a boy." Nephi elbowed her and raised one of his eyebrows.

"Just drive," Esther said. "I am sixteen."

"Baby," he said under his breath.

"Boy who can't grow a beard."

Sophie snorted. "Hey, my future limousine driver, you don't need to stay." She held out her cell and took a selfie of the three of them. Nephi crossed his eyes.

"Nice try, squirt." Nephi started his truck, turned on the lights, and ground the gears as he rounded the corner and took the main road to the cove. They parked a block away from the Captain Cove Mansion, next to an old green sedan.

"Check out the broken taillight on the sedan," Nephi said. "That's like having a sign on your car that says 'pull me over.'" He laughed.

Sophie looked at the little car. "Quiet, genius. Someone's in it."

"Oh, shoot!" Nephi laughed quietly. "They're probably going to the party."

Embarrassed, Esther turned her head and walked by as if she didn't see the man in the car.

They quickly passed the little car and moved silently together toward the woods and the private party.

Every window was lit up in the four-story mansion, outshining the stars in the clear night sky. They had strung white twinkle lights in the large trees lining the walk, to the front door, and along a path around the house to the backyard.

"We go through the trees here." Esther motioned for Nephi and Sophie to follow her.

"What does his dad do again?" Sophie asked.

"He runs the hospital," Nephi answered.

"No wonder they charged my dad a million dollars when I had to have stitches."

Esther held a finger to her lips and said, "Shush. I don't think his parents know we're here. I've never been in trouble in my life, and I am not about to start now. The last thing I need on my college application is a trespassing charge."

"Relax." Nephi gave her a little push. "You are such a good girl. You gotta learn to live a little."

Esther spun around and pushed him. "No, I don't!"

"Relax," he said again, holding his hands up.

"I can't relax. Bad things happen to people who do stuff like this. You know what? I'm going back to the truck." She walked past him. Her heart was pounding in her chest. She wanted to run, but he held her wrist.

"Esther . . . Esther . . . it's okay," Nephi hissed. "Parker's coming." He let go of her arm.

She turned around and saw Parker smiling and waving from the tree house ladder. He jumped down to the ground and came to meet them.

"Hey!" he called softly. "Welcome to our new clubhouse."

She couldn't believe the goofy grin on his face. He jogged easily in their direction and gave her and Sophie a quick hug. He smelled wonderful, like clean laundry and soap.

"Come on," he said, motioning for them to follow. "You'll love this." He climbed through the trapdoor and held it open for Nephi. Parker gave Nephi, and then Sophie, a hand up.

Esther stood at the base of the tree, still shaking. Unexplained anger coursed through her body. Whenever she was afraid, her body had a mind of its own and it chose fight over flight. It flooded her with adrenaline and anger, causing her to do and say things she regretted.

She didn't know why she felt this way or what triggered it, but if she wanted to, she was sure she could run the mountain two or three times. Parker just kept grinning at her, like a little boy. A beautiful, beautiful boy. The anger melted into the ground and was replaced with a different kind of fire.

She awkwardly climbed until his strong hands lifted her easily into the changed tree house. Parker must have worked all afternoon. In the middle of the tree house, he'd set up a tiny table with a clean white tablecloth and a beautiful candle inside a glass quart jar. There was a charcuterie board with meats, cheeses, and olives. He had fresh strawberries and pineapple dipped in dark chocolate on a silver tray. Cans of ginger ale were in a white bucket of ice.

"How did you get all this up here?" Esther asked.

"Who cares? This is awesome!" Sophie had a paper plate and began loading it with fruit.

"And I got a telescope," he announced.

"You rock," Sophie said, forgetting the food and going to the window. She began taking photos of everything, including a selfie with Parker.

"I also have some binoculars." He offered them to Esther, who still stood by the trapdoor, like a scared mouse.

*Did he hear us fighting? Was he watching?* Shame flooded through her, and she looked down. "Won't your parents be upset?"

"My dad knows. He's cool. He hates Mom's friends. He thinks they're pretentious and boring." Parker shrugged and went on. "But, we didn't tell Paisley. It would annoy her, and she might post it on social media."

"I thought you were twins. Don't you share everything?" Nephi asked.

Parker smiled. "Usually."

"Nephi's just sad she isn't here," Sophie said between bites of cheese.

Esther had finally relaxed. Parker had thought of everything. He had lined up folding lawn chairs along the window and offered Esther a stadium blanket. She brushed off her shorts and pulled the ponytail holder out of her hair, letting her long brown waves hang free. They all loaded up plates of food as limousines and other fancy vehicles pulled up to the mansion and valets drove them to the cove parking lot, trotting the half a block back to the party.

*Why is he so nice to me?*

Parker talked and laughed with Sophie as if they were old friends. He wasn't nearly as arrogant as Esther thought he was. With all his money and privilege, why was he hanging out with her? He could have anyone. He always had a girl following him. Everyone loved the Stuart twins. His sister, Paisley, had thousands of followers online. Everyone knew high-end shoe companies and a handbag manufacturer sponsored her. The kids at school all bet on which running shoe or exercise-wear company would pick her up.

A string quartet played on the mansion's back porch. The music carried to the gazebo, across the creek, and wandered through the tree house.

People eventually gathered at the tables while the caterer filled their glasses and delivered dinner salads to the impressive gathering. Fresh cut bouquets of flowers were everywhere, and a large flower arrangement made with driftwood, electric candles, and vintage silverware was suspended from the ceiling in the gazebo.

"How did your mother get a night without rain? There isn't a cloud in the sky." Sophie was looking intently through her dad's expensive binoculars hung by a strap around her neck. She had brought them for the occasion.

Parker was using something that looked like opera glasses. Esther wasn't sure but was too embarrassed to ask.

"Oh my gosh!" Sophie exclaimed, sitting forward in her seat. "That's Ransom Abram! He's so hot! He must be in the movie."

"I heard he might play the lead warlock," Parker said.

"Shut the front door." Sophie dropped the binoculars and grabbed Parker's arm.

"Serious." He laughed. "Wait until you see the head witch."

Just then, a lean woman with short gray hair and cat eyeglasses came out of the house and started walking toward the gazebo.

"Oh my goats! That's Lady White!" Sophie exclaimed.

Laughing even harder, Parker said, "Quiet. We don't want them to think we're the paparazzi."

Just then Paisley crossed the lawn with the black-haired girl from the book shop. Of course, Paisley looked perfect. She wore a navy striped maxi dress that accentuated her figure. On the other hand, her friend could have been straight out of a gothic novel. Her black dress came down straight to her knees and was met by black army boots laced with silver shoelaces. Her long sleeves were bell-shaped and looked like shredded lace.

Without a word, Paisley and her friend stopped on the steps of the gazebo and took a selfie with the celebrities behind them. Then they leaned into Ransom and snapped a picture of the three of them.

"Who's that?" Esther asked.

"Ransom," Parker answered.

"No, I mean the girl in black with Paisley. Is she an actress?"

"Oh." It was the first time Esther had seen Parker's smile go away. His shoulders fell, and his face clouded. "That's Bridget Merriweather."

"Madison's daughter! No one gets to see her." Excited, Sophie leaned out the open window. Esther worried she might pass out.

"She's a witch," Parker said.

"She's in the movie?" Sophie asked.

"No. I mean the real deal. The kind that makes your skin crawl." Parker sat forward and visibly frowned.

"Wow. What did she do to you?"

"Sophie!" Esther couldn't believe Sophie had asked.

"It's okay. She and Paisley have been fighting over Ransom. She's mean, not like Paisley. I heard her threaten Paisley if she didn't back off."

"Does Paisley like Ransom?" Nephi frowned.

"Who knows? He looks good in her pictures." Parker shrugged. "I have to go." He left through the trapdoor.

"Way to go, Sophie," Nephi said once Parker disappeared from view.

"What?"

"Parker used to date Bridget." Nephi didn't say any more. He didn't need to.

*Why does that bother me so much?* Esther wondered.

"Well, he can do better, like by dating Esther," Sophie said.

"Sophie!" Esther looked to see if Nephi was laughing. *Parker wouldn't want to date me.*

Without looking away from the party unfolding before them, Sophie pointed, "Look, there's Parker." She handed Esther the binoculars.

She looked. She didn't want to care, but she did. His long blond hair was loose and stood out against the black silk shirt he wore over jeans. Elegant. It was the only way to describe him. She examined her Oceanside hoodie and suddenly felt very uncomfortable.

"Well, we've seen it. Maybe we should go," Esther said.

"Are you kidding?" Sophie asked.

"Not a chance," Nephi said. "I'm meeting Paisley after the party. I'm asking her to the prom. Parker is giving you guys a ride home."

"I should have brought my homework." Esther shook her head. *All I have to do is break rules or fight and I'm miserable.*

"Seriously? Come on, Esther. We're witch hunting, remember? You don't want to miss this." As if on cue, the author Madison Merriweather made her late entrance to claps and welcomes from the party guests.

Sophie was so involved in watching the event unfold she didn't see Nephi pull his chair closer to Esther.

"Hey," he whispered. "Sorry."

"Me too." She looked at him. "I can't explain what comes over me. Sometimes I get so scared, like I will die. And when I do, something happens to me and I get angry, or I just freeze. I don't know what to do, so I do something stupid, like push you."

"It's okay." He put his arm around her shoulder and gave it a quick squeeze. "Don't get all sappy on me." He gave her his famous dimpled smile, the one that would get Paisley to say yes to the prom.

She couldn't help but grin back.

"You were a scared kid," he said.

Confused, she looked at him and cocked her head. "What do you mean?"

"When you and Grace came to live with us. Before Mary was born."

"You remember that?"

"Sure do. You took my bedroom with the cowboy wallpaper." He smiled again, but her mind was spinning, back to the room with the red cowboy hats and horses on the wall. "You were jumpy. All I had to do was say 'boo' and you would go running and crying to Grace. So I did it all the time."

She remembered. She didn't remember a lot about her childhood, but she remembered this.

"So, I should be the one who says I'm sorry. I probably ruined you for life," Nephi said.

"You aren't that important." She smiled at him and looked down at her feet. "I did that all on my own."

They were both silent for a minute, thinking.

"I've figured it out, though," she said. "People who are good live like Parker, right? Good things happen to good people. I just have to be good, graduate college, and, you know, not be poor like Mom. I'll do it all differently."

Nephi studied her for a minute and then shook his head. "I hope you aren't that different from Grace. Being poor doesn't mean you're bad. Grace is the best."

"Yeah, but we'll be rich," Sophie said. Esther didn't know she was listening. The serious energy broke, and they went back to watching Sophie slobber over the famous people.

Esther couldn't remember talking to Nephi like that before. But then, they hadn't been stuck alone in a tree house without video games before.

Below, Paisley left the gazebo and walked back toward the house. Nephi leaned forward in his chair.

"I'm going to get closer and see if I can talk to Paisley." He gave her a goofy grin.

"Nephi!" Esther stood up to stop him, but he was already to the door. She leaned over and the trapdoor and said, "You're going to get Parker in trouble and get us thrown out of here."

He looked up from the bottom of the ladder. "Nah. I got this. Don't worry. I'll be back."

# 8

# Be on Your Best Behavior

The party was over. Sophie and Esther waited in the tree house for Nephi or Parker to return. They sat in lawn chairs facing the window while Sophie rattled on about the party.

An odd waiter in a wrinkled white shirt and gray slacks picked up the last flower arrangement and carried it around to the front of the house. Esther thought he looked different from the other smartly pressed waiters and waitresses.

Finally, Parker came out of the mansion's back door, crossed the lawn, and easily leapt over the fence. The last caterer carried chairs to their van in the driveway, and Esther heard it pull away. The house lights in the mansion went off, one by one, darkening all the windows.

Parker climbed into the tree house smiling. He gave Esther a quick hug and listened to Sophie gush while he gathered up the dishes and stacked everything in a basket he had hidden under the table. Esther silently helped him fold the white tablecloth. Neither of them tried to talk while Sophie rattled on.

"You should see some of the great pictures I got. I want to see the pictures Paisley took in the gazebo." Sophie sat down and searched social media for party photos posted by Paisley, Madison Merriweather, or one of the other celebrities in attendance. She turned around, held her phone up, and smiled. Her cell flashed while she took one, two, three selfies. She adjusted her settings and took a few without the flash.

In the quiet they heard a screen door slam and then a woman's voice. "I'm so sick of the way you treat my friends, Robert!" Parker's mom yelled at her husband. Everyone in the tree house froze.

"Well, I'm sick of your friends drinking everything in the house and taking up all our time, without ever reciprocating! This is costing us a fortune, and I still have all the expenses on the family home in England."

"You mean that drafty castle? You should have rented that out years ago!"

Stunned, Esther and Parker walked side by side to the tree house window and watched his parents fight in the backyard. It unfolded so fast. Esther looked at Parker, who watched mouth open and his eyes wide. It was like coming up on a gruesome car accident. You couldn't look away, but you couldn't stop watching. She didn't know what to do.

"Seriously, Mel? I came to America for you! I bought this house for you! Those ten-thousand-dollar shoes on your feet came from me because I love you."

"Here we go again! Listing everything I've spent for the last year. Why do you hold it against me?" Parker's mother shouted and folded her arms.

Parker leaned out the window. All the color drained from his face. With eyes wide open, horrified, he watched his parents, his white knuckled hands prying away pieces of the window trim.

"I don't want to fight," Parker's father said.

"Well, I do. I want my own life."

"What are you saying? Are you trying to destroy me? This is a small town, and they hired a chief executive officer *and* his wife! You're part of the package. You wanted to be the wife of an executive. A regular doctor wasn't good enough. We built this life together."

"I don't care." She started walking back to the house. He crossed the lawn and grabbed her by the arm and spun her around to look at him. She slapped him, hard.

He seemed stunned. His face darkened, and he stepped back and pointed at her. "You won't leave me. I won't let you."

Parker gasped and jerked back a step. Esther grabbed his arm and turned away, but she had to look back.

"You can't control me!" Parker's mother tried to slap his father again. He caught her arm before her hand touched his right cheek. She swiped at his face with her left hand, leaving red scratch marks bleeding on his cheek. He let go of her and put his hand on his face and swore. She turned and stalked into the house. He only hesitated for a moment before following her.

Esther was frozen, heart pounding and gripping Parker's arm. When it was over and she started to come to, she looked at Parker, whose mouth hung open, his eyes round. He was shaking his head. He stuttered, "I am . . . I . . . I can't believe . . . I am so sorry you saw that."

Esther exhaled when she realized she was holding her breath. Her whole body was vibrating. She looked down at her shaking hands, and then at Parker who was shaking his head, one hand in his pocket, looking at the floor. Any color he had had drained from his face.

Sophie stood with her mouth open but was unusually silent, holding her cell phone.

Parker hadn't been talking about *her* parents not getting along when he'd offended her at the bookstore. He was talking about *his*, and this wasn't the first time.

"I am so sorry . . . " Esther started to say.

His shoulders slumped, and she felt her words only made it worse.

"Well, I'm not," Sophie said. They both looked at her, confused. "At least they're speaking. Better than the cold war at my house."

Parker smiled weakly, but his eyes were moist, and he shuddered. "I should go down there."

"Everybody's parents fight. They'll make up any minute and it'll be disgusting. Trust me, Parker, we all understand and are here for you," Sophie said.

Parker looked at them and smiled, relieved not to be alone.

Hesitantly, Esther said, "Well, at least your dad didn't attempt to kidnap you and isn't writing you from prison."

With his eyes still moist, he shook his head and wrapped the two girls in a hug.

"I'm suffocating. You're built like a brick!" Sophie said into his chest. He let go, and they all laughed, the strangeness between them gone. They had something in common—dysfunctional families.

"Come on, I'll clean this up in the morning. Let me give you a ride home. I need to go check on Paisley."

Parker waited for Esther under the tree house. Her feet searched in the dark for the wood nailed to the trunk. At least her legs were long. She don't know how Sophie did it.

*I should have worn my glasses. It's hard to see in the dark.*

Esther's long hair kept falling in her face. When she got close to the ground, Parker put his hands around her small waist, and she jumped the rest of the way. He did the same for Sophie. Esther pushed her hair out of her face. Parker turned on the light on his cell phone and used it like a flashlight. No one spoke.

They walked in his phone's pool of light, making their way through the woods. At the edge of the forest, the street lamp made it easier to navigate.

When they got to the front of the house, Paisley came out onto the front lawn. Nephi followed her. Esther heard him say, "It's going to be all right," and then he reached out to touch her shoulder. She shook her head and pulled away. Turning to look at him, her face clouded over and her bottom lip trembled. She had dressed in black spandex running gear and had their dog, General Cornwallis, on a leash. She took a deep breath and without a word turned and walked toward the cove. Nephi started to follow her. She glared at him over her shoulder and he stopped, hands on his hips, watching her go.

Bridget left the house right behind them and got into a black sports car, which seemed to match her mood. She was frowning, with a headphone in one ear. She sped off.

"Wow, should we leave Paisley alone?" Sophie asked. Paisley picked up her pace and started running toward the cove.

"Everyone copes with Mum and Dad's tiffs any way they can." Parker waived at Nephi, who jogged across the lawn and joined them at the gate.

"I can give the girls a ride home," Nephi said.

"Thanks, mate." Parker looked down at his feet.

"Cheerio," Sophie said and slapped Parker on the back.

Parker looked at Esther and gathered her into another quick hug. "Thanks," he whispered and, after letting go, walked with his head down into the house.

"Man. Did you hear Parker's parent's fight?" Nephi asked.

"Nope." Esther walked toward the truck.

"Do you think I should delete the picture of it?" Sophie asked.

✦ ✦ ✦

They rode home in silence. Nephi parked the truck in the driveway and turned it off. No one moved.

"Well, that happened," Sophie said.

"Sophie!" Esther scolded her.

"You can't ignore it, Esther. Paisley, Bridget, and I saw the whole thing," Nephi said. "She's really embarrassed. I'm worried about her. What if they split up? Bridget said her parents split. Does anyone stay together anymore?"

"The Ironpots," Esther said softly. They were the couple she thought about when she thought about good marriages. The dream family.

"Should we tell your mom?" Sophie asked.

"No!" Esther felt a jolt of fear run through her. "She's a domestic violence advocate. She'd want to do something. Then everyone would know. Parker would never forgive me or any of us. Did you see how embarrassed he was?"

"Yeah, but she hit him. He had a big red mark on his face," Sophie said.

"She's half his size," Nephi retorted.

"It doesn't matter! I don't care if he is a woman and she is a man—no one should hit anyone. Wait, that didn't sound right." Sophie tried again. "I mean it's abuse."

"It wasn't that bad," Esther said. "And it's none of our business."

"Not that bad?" Sophie looked shocked. Then a look of understanding crossed her face. "Oh, I get it. Compared to you—"

Before she could finish, Nephi opened the truck door and ended the conversation when he asked, "So, are you sleeping over, Sophie?"

Esther answered, "Yes, and we're eating all the ice cream. Want to join us?"

"Can I pick the movie?"

"No way!" Sophie shook her head. "I am not watching another everything-gets-blown-up-and-a-bunch-of-aliens movie."

"What do you want to watch?" Nephi asked.

# 9

# Because I Said So

"We're home!" Esther's mom, Grace, announced.

Esther woke from a sound sleep and sat up, trying to get her eyes to focus. The morning sun was streaming in through the open front door. She was on one end of her mother's cream-colored couch with chocolate ice cream on the coffee table and, she remembered, on the front of her T-shirt. Popcorn was everywhere. They had been throwing it at each other sometime during the night.

"What happened here?" Hart was standing behind Grace with suitcases. He dropped them, hard.

Grace patted him on the shoulder. "Relax. Get used to it."

"Okay, you guys, clean it up," Grace said, stepping gingerly through the chaos and heading up the stairs with Hart following her.

"Welcome home," Grandma Mable called from the top of the stairs.

"Mommy!" Esther's little sister, Mary, ran across the floor upstairs.

The blanket on the other end of the couch moved, and Sophie peeked out. "Are they gone?"

Esther threw a pillow at her and laughed. "Yes. Help me clean up this mess."

Nephi stood up from the floor in front of the fireplace, scratched his stomach, and stretched.

"My mother would have killed me if she had come into a mess like this," Sophie said.

Esther chuckled. "She trusts us."

"We got her fooled." Nephi shuffled off toward the door to Grandma Mable's apartment and his loft bedroom in the back part of Esther's house. The apartment was hidden neatly behind a door that looked like a wardrobe and the way to Narnia.

"Hey! You're not getting out of cleaning up," Esther said, with her hands on her hips.

"I just got to go to the bathroom." He yawned and went through the door.

Somewhere in the mess, a phone started ringing. Both girls frantically threw blankets and popcorn until Esther found it. It was Nephi's.

"It's Parker." She held up the screen to show Sophie.

"Answer it."

"Should I?"

"Hurry up!" Sophie exclaimed.

"Hello?" Esther asked.

"Esther?" Parker asked. "I thought this was Nephi's number."

"No. Yes. This is Nephi's phone. He just went . . . Well, do you want me to get him? Is everything okay?" Esther could hear Parker's rapid breath on the other end of the line. His breathing was interrupted by a jagged deep breath and the hair raised on the back of her neck. *Is he crying?*

"It's just . . . well, something happened . . . " Parker let out his breath in a whoosh. "Paisley and my mum are missing."

"What? Missing?" Esther said. She heard her blood pumping like a waterfall of white noise. Her mind raced but no two thoughts lined up coherently. *Where's my mom? I saw her hit him. I'm cold . . .*

"Police are here and they're talking to my dad. Is your mom back yet? They're talking about calling someone. I just excused myself, and well, I want it to be your mum. I trust you guys," Parker said in a rush. He sounded frantic.

"I don't know how it works." Esther couldn't think. "They just call her. I can ask my grandma. Wait, I hear something."

Esther heard someone on the stairs and then the sound of her mother's voice speaking to Mary. "I'll be back. Be good for Hart. Maybe he'll walk you to town for donuts." With that, her sister squealed, and her mom came the rest of the way down the stairs.

"Esther," her mom said. "I have to go. I am already back on the clock for work." She rolled her eyes.

"Mom. Mom. You need to go to the Stuarts' house?" Esther grabbed her mother's arm.

Her mom stopped, a confused look on her face. "Why . . . ?" she asked slowly. "Esther, you're shaking. What happened?"

"I want to go with you. We need to go."

"You know I can't take you to work with me. What's going on, Esther? Sophie? Tell me."

"Parker is Nephi's best friend. We have to make sure Parker's okay." She didn't tell her mother that Parker was still on the phone listening to the whole conversation, but she put her hand over the phone as if she could muffle her voice and said quietly through gritted teeth, "His mother is missing and so is his sister, Paisley. I saw . . . " She stopped herself.

Her mother's eye narrowed and she looked from Esther to Sophie and back to Esther. She tilted her head and studied her. She gently put her arm around Esther's shaking shoulders and said firmly, "Esther. Everything I do is confidential. You know that. I can't tell you where I'm going or who I'm talking to, so don't ask. And if for some reason someone says anything to you, don't repeat it. Now, please, could you just clean up, take some deep breaths, and relax? I'm sure they are getting help. Okay?"

"But what about Parker?"

"I'm sure Parker will tell Nephi if he wants to. But it is not your place, and it certainly isn't mine." With that, she walked out the door, and Esther heard the old SUV start.

Esther looked at Sophie and then remembered the phone in her hand. "Parker?"

"I heard."

Hope came down the stairs with her stuff packed to go back to Grandma Mable's apartment, after sleeping in Mary's room, so Mary could stay with Mable during the honeymoon. "Hey," she said. Her brows drew together, her eyes narrowed, and she dropped her bags on the floor.

"Hey," Esther replied. She her back on Hope, and whispered into the phone, "Do you want me to get Nephi?"

"Yes. Wait. Guess I should be okay if your mom is coming. I'm okay." His jagged breathing was interrupted by a loud exhale and sniff.

"You don't sound okay." She closed her eyes and tried to slow her own breathing.

Sophie took the phone out of Esther's hand. "We're on our way. Uh-huh. You're welcome." She ended the call and handed it back to Esther. "Get some clothes on. We're not leaving him to do this alone."

"Who are you, masked woman, and what have you done with Sophie?" *I love her strength.*

"I'm an only child, and I know what being alone is really like, so get dressed, and let's go. Do you have a shirt I can borrow?"

Nephi walked back into the room.

"You're never going to believe what just happened," Sophie said. "You better get dressed quick."

"Wait, I'll drop you off," Hope said. "I've got the keys to Hart's old SUV. He's letting me drive it to work today. I can get you there faster. Now tell me what's going on."

They parked by the same little green sedan they had seen the night before down the road from Parker's house. They wanted to stay out of sight in case Esther's mother was already there.

"Seriously, whose car is that?" Esther asked. "I swear that's the guy that was bugging Paisley at the Madison Merriweather's party." She stopped and tried to remember more details from the book signing. "Sophie, didn't he photo bomb one of your selfies?" Her heart had stopped racing, but she was still alert. She pushed her glasses up and then took them off and cleaned them for the fifth time as she reviewed the events of the evening before, over and over.

"I don't know who they are," Nephi said. "But they have a rocking camera in the front seat. Take a look at that camera lens. You could take a close-up from a mile away. That's an expensive piece of equipment to leave in an unlocked car."

"Should we be nice and lock it for them?" Esther asked.

"In this small town?" Hope chuckled. "It's fine. Let's go."

When they were close to the house, Nephi put his arm out, holding up his hand to stop them, and said, "Maybe you girls should stay outside. I don't want to overwhelm him." A Necanicum police car was parked on the curb.

"No way." Sophie put her hands on her hips and shook her head.

"We want to help," Hope said. "I have the keys to Hart's old SUV and have some time before I have to go to work. I wonder if Hart is working today."

"What are we going to call him? Joe? Hart? Dad sounds weird," Esther said.

"If we let Hope drive us anywhere again, we won't need to worry about it. Hand over the keys," Nephi said.

Hope smiled and jingled them in his face. Nephi tried to grab the keys, but Hope was too fast for him. She tucked them into her pocket.

When they reached the house, they began walking around to the back.

"Do you think he noticed we didn't have any surfboards?" Sophie asked.

Esther chuckled. "The honeymooner? Not at all. Did you text Parker, Nephi?"

"Yeah. I told him we would meet him around back, at the door to the study. His dad is talking to the police."

"They have a study?" Esther asked.

"Now is not the time to geek out on books," Sophie pointed out. "Unless they have . . . "

"Shh." Hope put a finger to her lips and pointed at two police officers coming out of the back of the old mansion through a pair of French doors.

A young-looking officer stopped on the edge of the generous back porch and looked out across the lawn. The older officer took a pack of cigarettes out of his wrinkled shirt pocket and lit one with a silver lighter. Taking a puff, he blew the smoke away from his coworker.

Esther motioned for everyone to crouch to avoid being caught. They were close enough to hear the officers talking but were hidden by a manicured rhododendron.

"What do you think?" the younger officer asked the older officer.

He blew out smoke, pushed his police cap back on his head, and looked across the lawn. He took one more puff. "Well, whatever happened isn't good. Detective Kohornen will be in charge when he gets here. Mr. Stuart has scratches on his face that could be defensive wounds. He's definitely got the money to make them disappear. I hear he's an earl or a lord or something over in England. It wouldn't be the first time a man got rid of his family."

"But what about the son? Why leave the son behind to call us?" the young officer asked.

"This might be your first homicide." The older officer used his free hand to adjust his belt around his girth. "Your job is to observe and not touch anything. Take careful notes of everything you see or hear. Keep your mouth shut. Follow me and don't walk on anything that I don't. The detective will be here soon." He flicked the glowing cigarette into the flower bed and went into the house, with the younger officer following closely.

Sophie pulled a leaf out of her hair. They stood and saw Parker motioning to them from another set of French doors that also opened onto the large back porch.

Parker's eyes had dark circles under them. His normally perfect hair looked slept on and then gathered in a ponytail. He had on a plain gray hoodie and jeans.

Esther was immediately in love with the room he invited them into. It was filled with books and felt wise and almost haunted. The ceiling had a stained glass inset in the center. The room was completely circled by a balcony of more books.

Parker invited them across the room to a grouping of couches surrounding a warm fire burning under a stately mantel. Other than bookshelves, there was another narrow door tucked behind an ornate iron spiral staircase leading to the balcony.

Esther wanted to take it all in, but Parker's sad face kept her attention. His eyes were scanning her face. He rocked on his feet and looked down at the floor, and then folded his arms.

Nephi gathered Parker in a side-by-side man hug with a back pat. Sophie jumped into the middle of them, and Parker pulled her in. To Esther's surprise, he wiped his eyes over Nephi's shoulder.

"Thanks, guys." Parker looked at the floor. Nephi stepped back and smacked Parker's back one more time.

"I'm glad you're here, but I don't know if my dad will okay with it. He's meeting with the police in the living room. He's pretty upset," Parker said.

"You mean there are more rooms than this?" Sophie asked. Nephi elbowed Sophie.

Parker went on. "I don't know what they're waiting for, but they've been here since I called at about seven this morning. Dad's mad they aren't out looking for Paisley and Mum."

"Why did you call them?" Hope asked.

"I called first because I couldn't find Cornwallis. That's our dog. I thought he might have been picked up by the animal control officer," Parker explained to Hope. "I realized he was missing when I got up to walk him. After I called the police asking for animal control, I remembered Paisley had taken him on her run last night, so I went to her room to check. Her bed wasn't slept in. Bridget was in the guest bed in her suite but wasn't any help."

"Does she know where Paisley is?" Esther asked.

"She said she hadn't seen her all night. She said Ransom—you know, the movie star—had asked Paisley out last night. Maybe she's still with him, but that wouldn't be like her. She'd never stay out all night." Parker raised one eyebrow and shrugged, unsure.

"With Ransom?" Nephi hissed.

"Now, now, big boy," Sophie said. "This isn't all about you."

Nephi nodded and shoved his hands deep into his pockets scowling.

"The officers don't sound that concerned, but Dad and I are terrified. This isn't normal. And I have this feeling, like something's wrong, you know?" Parker brows drew together, and he shook his head, looking down.

"Yes. Trust your gut." Esther put a hand on his shoulder. He looked into her eyes, and they exchanged a look of understanding.

"I better get back out there." Parker looked nervously at the door to the study.

"Leave the door open so we can hear what's going on," Sophie whispered.

"Sophie." Esther shook her head.

"No. She's right," Parker said. "Nephi, you're the first person I thought of. I don't know what I would do without you." He gave Esther's hand a squeeze, and she felt her heart beat faster. He let go and slipped out the door.

He was back in seconds. "They're coming this way. Quick! Get into the bathroom." He started pushing Nephi with the girls following toward the door on the far side of the room. It led to a small lavatory off the study. He closed two doors to the bathroom. It looked like it led another into a hallway. "Quiet!" was the last thing he whispered before closing the study door.

The room was a half bath with a sink, toilet, and another narrow oak door. There were two large ferns in gold pots on either side of the toilet, taking up space. It was small enough they were cramped and unsure of where to stand. Esther backed awkwardly into the sink and tried to adjust herself so she wasn't stepping on Sophie and her elbow wasn't in Nephi's stomach.

"Now what?" Esther asked.

"We listen." Sophie put her finger to her lips to tell them to be quiet as she turned the door handle, letting the door open, just a crack.

Sophie held the door handle so there was just space enough to see the sitting area. Hope knelt and peered under Sophie. Esther leaned over Sophie to see out, and Nephi was tall enough to find space at the small opening.

"They'll catch us," Nephi whispered.

"They will if you keep talking! Now be quiet!" Sophie said.

Parker's dad took a seat on an old-fashioned sofa near the large fireplace, too close to the bathroom door for comfort. The back was hand-carved, and the cushions were faded blue velvet. Sitting by Parker, Mr. Stuart draped his arm over his son and then pulled him in. He looked as tired as Parker did. He massaged his scalp with his free hand and then took his arm off Parker and ran both hands through his hair, until it stuck up. He sighed deeply.

The officer with the wrinkled shirt stood silently by the door to the living room. Esther heard a sharp knock on the wooden door. The officer opened it and then let in a tall, lean man in a suit. His hair was brown and clean cut. He looked like he had just left church.

The older officer who had been smoking on the deck said, "Mr. Stuart, this is Detective Kohornen."

The detective's face was soft and round. His only truly unique feature was a pair of unusually large ears that made his round face look wider.

"Don't let his soft face fool you," the older officer went on as if he could read Esther's mind. "He is Officer Kohornen's son and one bright cookie and tough as they come. They raised him for this job."

"Thanks, Officer Neilson," Kohornen said.

"No offense, Detective, but why aren't you out looking for my wife and daughter?" Mr. Stuart asked.

Parker leaned forward and put his face in his hands, frowning. He looked up at the fireplace.

Esther was afraid to breathe. *What is wrong with us? We're going to get into trouble. But look at him. He needs us.*

Sophie whispered, "Nephi, don't use my head like an armrest."

"Sorry," he replied quietly and adjusted himself.

The junior officer entered the room and whispered something in the detective's ear.

"Well, tell her just a minute," Detective Kohornen replied and looked annoyed. "I want to talk to her first." The young officer nodded and went back out the way he came in.

The detective took out a pad of paper and a small recorder. "Mr. Stuart, we'd like to record our interview. Do you understand, and is that acceptable?"

"I don't care! But you need to find them. My wife wouldn't go anywhere without her things. And Paisley wouldn't ever leave behind her car and her purse. Something has happened, Detective!" Mr. Stuart's face was bright red against his blue shirt. He ran his fingers through his blond hair again and then rubbed his face. He started to pace.

"Listen, Mr. Stuart, I have a domestic violence advocate from the Family Crisis Center waiting on the back porch. Her job is to support you. Let me get your interview over with and introduce you to the advocate so we can get out there and find your wife and daughter."

"I'm not a victim," Mr. Stuart said.

Parker looked at the bathroom door and then anxiously at his father. "Dad, let them help us. We need them to look for Mum and Paisley. And please, let me help."

"I'm sorry, son," Detective Kohornen said. "But we need to speak to your dad alone for a few minutes."

"Is anyone out there looking yet?" Parker stood to leave, shoulders slumped.

"Trust us, Parker. We're all invested in finding your family members, but we have to avoid wasting the department's and county's valuable time."

*What does he think he's doing? Get on with it!* Esther thought.

Parker left the study by the living room door.

"If you'll excuse me, Mr. Stuart, I need to brief the advocate." The detective left the room, with the recorder running on the table.

The handle to the other door in the bathroom moved. Parker opened it, to everyone's relief, and joined them. They made way for him to have the best view of the study.

After a few tense minutes, the detective returned with Esther's mom.

The detective said, "This is Grace James. She's an advocate with the Family Crisis Center. She . . . "

Mr. Stuart interrupted. "I don't need an advocate. I have my attorney on retainer."

"I know but I'm required to offer support for your family," Detective Kohornen explained. He nodded at Grace, indicating she had the floor.

"Mr. Stuart, I'm not an attorney. My job is to take care of you, even after the police leave, to continue to support you twenty-four-seven while things are progressing, and to keep everything you say to me confidential. I'm here to help." Grace had circles under her eyes from her recent flight, but she didn't move. She waited quietly for what felt to Esther like forever.

Finally, Mr. Stuart breathed out and looked at Grace. "All right. Thank you for being here."

"While they interview you, I can't speak. I am just here to listen, so you only have to tell the story once," Grace explained.

Mr. Stuart looked confused. He opened his mouth as if he was going to say something and then, as if he had second thoughts, closed it and gestured for the detective to continue.

Esther turned to Parker and whispered, "Shouldn't his attorney be here for the interview?"

Parker's brows drew together, and he shrugged. "I don't know."

The detective picked up his recorder and noted the date and time and listed everyone he knew who was present in the room.

He noted on the recording that the interview was regarding Melissa Stuart and Paisley Stuart, who were both reported missing less than twenty-four hours ago, along with their labradoodle, Cornwallis. After adding various facts like the address, he said, "Mr. Stuart, can you tell me your full name?"

"Robert Parker Stuart. What good does all this do? Shouldn't you be asking about my wife? Or about Paisley? Paisley is online all the time. I checked, and she hasn't posted since last night. She could be in real danger. There are a lot of dangerous people out there."

"There are facts we need to collect, Mr. Stuart." The detective made a note in a small flipbook. "Can you tell me what happened?"

"We had an argument last night, a typical married couple argument, that's all. Then, when I got up this morning, she was gone. She took almost nothing. No note, nothing. You see, that's the thing! Mel left her wallet. Her purse, her phone, and her wallet are all in the bedroom and laid out on her dresser."

"Isn't it possible they just went for a walk? After all, it's only about ten in the morning," the detective asked.

"No! You don't know my wife. Hot yoga, maybe. A massage, definitely. A walk? Not unless it was in a major shopping mall."

"I thought your daughter was a runner, and the photos on the grand piano in the living room show your wife and daughter dressed alike at a track meet."

"Paisley is a runner," Mr. Stuart said. "She was running last night, as a matter of fact. But her mother, Mel, was just volunteering at the high school race. She uses a gym in town. She likes classes, like yoga or cycling."

"Doesn't she ride? Wasn't there a photo of your wife riding a horse?" The detective cocked his head and raised an eyebrow.

"She hasn't ridden since we left England."

"I see. Can I ask a more personal question, Mr. Stuart? Do you and your wife often sleep apart?" The detective let the question hang heavy in the air.

Mr. Stuart looked at his feet and shook his head, shoulders slumped. Then he fell back into the big soft sofa and put his hand over his eyes. "Look. We've been under tremendous pressure since we came to your country. We have only had trouble recently. I've been under a lot of stress and working late. She needs her sleep or . . . " His voice trailed off.

"Or?" The detective waited, pen poised.

Mr. Stuart sighed and shook his head. "I think I need my attorney."

"Okay. This interview is terminated. But you should know we will have a harder time looking for them without your help. In fact, they haven't been gone very long. For all we know they are together and after the argument last night have left you. We usually wait at least a day before we launch a search like the one I think you are asking for. Just because you have money doesn't mean you should get any preferential treatment from me or any other law enforcement agency."

"They can't leave. We need someone to find her," Parker said. "Wait, don't leave!" he said as he pushed the bathroom door open, causing Sophie to fall onto the hardwood floor in the study. Esther nearly tripped trying to get untangled. She looked back to see Nephi frozen, one foot on the toilet and a look of horror on his face. Hope came out and checked on Sophie.

Grace stood. Her mouth fell open. "Esther!"

"Hi, Mom," Esther said, giving a shy wave.

"Excuse me." Grace marched toward Esther and Nephi and pushed all the kids back into the bathroom. Nephi opened the door to the hallway to give them space, while Grace shut the door to the study. "What are you all doing here? I told you not to come here."

Esther froze. All of her life, she had been good. "I . . . I . . . "

"No, you didn't," Sophie broke in. "You said not to tell anyone anything about your work. We're here for Parker." She patted Parker on the arm and smiled.

"Sonoko Ito, you knew better," Grace said to Sophie.

"Whoa! The whole name." Nephi chuckled.

"And you! Nephi Albert."

"Albert?" Parker asked and actually laughed.

Parker took Esther's hand. Her eyes got big and so did her mother's. She didn't miss a thing. Then he put his hand on Nephi's tall shoulder. "Mrs. James, I asked them to come and support me. I needed friends."

"They know it isn't safe to show up at homes where I'm working," Grace said.

*Ouch.*

Parker's face clouded. He was squeezing her hand so hard it hurt, but she wasn't about to move. His energy was fierce.

"My dad didn't hurt my mother. My mum and dad love each other. Paisley and Mum are in trouble. I feel it," he said. "My parents never fought before we moved here."

Esther looked at him, listened, and studied him. *Do I believe him?*

Parker went on, "We were happy in England. Life was good. Dad's been under a lot of pressure, and Mum is spending more time with her friends than she ever has before. It's Madison Merriweather. Mum didn't have such a large social circle before."

"I believe you. You don't talk like someone raised with . . . well . . . violence. But telling me that your mom was isolated from her friends in England doesn't make me feel better. Listen, Parker," Grace said and then looked around the room. "You're surrounded by some of the best kids in town. I happen to love them like they're my own. One of them is! Can you promise me—swear to me—they're safe here? You've never been in danger? You don't know what happened to Paisley?" She let out a long sigh.

Parker looked down but didn't answer.

"Come out." Grace held the door to the study open.

One by one, they shuffled out of the closet-sized bathroom. Sophie waved weakly at the detective, whose mouth fell open as the kids kept coming. They waited nervously in front of the fireplace with Parker.

The detective shook his head and checked to make sure the tape recorder was off. "Listen, I have a job to do. Grace, get these kids out of here. Neilson! I thought you were watching the perimeter. How did they get in?"

It wasn't really a question, and Officer Neilson didn't answer it. He shrugged and put his hands on his utility belt.

Grace directed the kids to the living room door and out of the library. They entered a large entryway. The library door opened underneath sweeping stairs that must have made up a grand entryway. They could see a small hallway that ran the length of the study, with narrow doors to rooms on the front of the house. It ended at the other door to the small bathroom.

"We'll wait right here. I promise," Sophie said to Grace and held up her pinky. "Pinky promise."

"Thanks, Sophie." Grace went back into the study, leaving them alone in the entryway.

"Come on." Sophie pulled Esther down the hall toward the bathroom.

"Sophie! We can't." Esther was appalled.

"No risk, no glory," Sophie said.

"I think that's no guts, no glory." Nephi smiled at Sophie.

"Guys." Parker stopped them dead in their tracks. They all looked at him. "I don't want you to get into trouble for helping me."

"Oh, come on!" Hope said. "What are they going to do to us? We're kids, and this is your house. Dude! We need to know what they're saying."

It was decided, and they went back to their listening post in the bathroom. Esther watched them go nervously and then reluctantly followed Parker. *I am going to be grounded for life.*

"Now that we have her description, we want your permission to talk to your son and to search the house," Detective Kohornen said.

"Whatever it takes, Officer." Mr. Stuart sounded deflated.

Grace said, "Mr. Stuart, I'd like to take some time to talk to you, if you don't mind. Is there somewhere we can talk in private?"

"I guess we could go out to the gazebo."

"Perfect." Grace stood. "Thank you for calling me, Detective."

As they left through the French doors, the kids quickly pushed each other and sprinted down the hall to the other door, where they tried to look casual as if they'd been waiting.

The door to the study opened.

"Parker," Detective Kohornen said, "I'd like to talk to you."

Without looking back, Parker walked like a man to his hanging. The door shut, and they stepped closer to the study door. Sophie gently pushed it open just enough for them to watch.

Neilson stood near the fireplace mantel. Detective Kohornen sat down and turned on the recorder, stated the date, and listed everyone in the room. At first, his questions were simple. He asked Parker's full name, about school, and some questions about being a twin. The detective even asked how Parker knew Esther. She froze, while Parker explained that Nephi, her uncle, was his friend.

"Esther's awesome," Parker said. He explained that they saw his parents' argument from the tree house.

"Look, kid. I know you're not telling the truth. I need to know if your dad and mom fight and if those fights get physical. For all we know, your mom just left your father and left you behind."

Parker jumped to his feet, hands fisted, and shouted, "You're not listening to me! My dad and mum don't fight like that. Sure, sometimes they argue, but they have never hit each other. Paisley's phone is here. Her car keys are here. Something is wrong."

"Parents who hit each other don't usually do it in front of the kids. You don't know what they do when you're not looking." The detective stood to leave.

"You haven't looked at all. At the least, retrace their steps. You didn't even talk to Bridget!" Parker shouted.

"Hey, now . . . Wait. Is Bridget Merriweather here?" Detective Kohornen asked.

"She's probably still sleeping," Parker said. The detective sat and gave Officer Neilson a look.

Kohornen asked through gritted teeth, "Neilson, can you go get the witness, Bridget Merriweather, if you can spare the time?"

"Sure thing. Sorry, sir." Neilson left the study.

"Thank you, Parker. We'll let you know if we have any more questions." The detective dismissed Parker.

"If you won't do anything, I will." Parker strode out of the room, without even trying to hide his frustration. He pushed open the living room door. "Let's go." He held his hand out to Esther.

She felt her heart race as she took his hand and he pulled her through the house and out the front door. Sophie, Nephi, and Hope followed. Parker walked off the porch and to the side of the house, where there was a three-car garage alongside the main structure. They gathered near the garage door.

Parker said, "The police are a waste of time. We need to look for Paisley. I know she went running that way." He pointed down his street, which turned toward the cove. "But I don't know if she came home. Dad thinks she did because her running shoes are on the floor in her room, but she owns a dozen pairs."

"What can we do?" Esther asked.

"Name it," Nephi said. "We're here for you."

"I need to wait for them to finish talking to Dad. Would you guys walk the shore and look for any sign of Paisley? I would think she would stay on the road, but who knows. It was a pretty bright night out. She might have tried to run the beach in the dark."

Parker grew very still, looking out at the horizon. He folded his arms as if he was holding himself. He took a step back from the group and looked toward the cove, silent.

In a quiet voice, he said, "What . . . What if she got caught . . . you know, by the surf?" He studied Nephi's face, brows drawn together, eyes moist, and then closed them.

Nephi gave him a pat on the shoulder. "We got this. Don't go there, dude. Text us when you're done."

Parker remained quiet, looking at Nephi first, then Esther, and finally at Hope and Sophie. He let out a deep breath. "I really appreciate it. What would I do without . . . ? "

Unable to restrain herself, Esther gave him a quick hug. "You don't have to find out. We won't give up. We'll look at her social media. Maybe she's posted something."

"We can do this, Parker," Sophie said in a serious tone.

"Thanks." Parker continued to stand quietly, looking out to sea.

"Get back in there, but stay in touch," Hope said. "And, Parker? You're not alone. We promise. You've got us to help you."

Parker wiped his face with the back of his hand and quietly went back inside.

# 10

# Be Careful or Your Face Will Stay That Way

"We should tell Mom we're leaving to look for Paisley at the beach," Esther said.

"Seriously, Esther?" Nephi replied.

"It's the right thing to do. I'll go to the gazebo and let her know we're headed out. It won't take but a second." Esther walked around the side of the house to the backyard.

She found the gazebo was empty, so she headed for the French doors to the study. She was about to open the doors when she heard the detective's voice. Then she heard a girl's voice she didn't recognize.

"He's a jerk. He got rid of her. I'm sure. He doesn't let Paisley do anything. He's so controlling. Isn't that a symptom? Ransom wanted her to go out with us, and her father said no. She was beside herself. He doesn't want Paisley or her mother to have any fun with anyone besides the family," the girl said.

"Why don't you leave the detective work to the police, Bridget?" Detective Kohornen asked. "Those are some pretty serious accusations."

"Well, they're true! Paisley heard her parents fighting. We watched the whole thing. It was like something off a television reality show. I tried to film it, but she stopped me. She hates them. That's why she went for a run," Bridget said. "I took a drive to cool off. I wanted to call Ransom."

"What time did she come back?"

"I don't know. I had taken my anti-anxiety sleeping pills, and my sleeping mask was on, and my earplugs were in."

Esther heard movement, someone walking on the hardwood floor. She withdrew from the door with her back against the wall. She was close enough she could still hear but wouldn't get caught if they looked her way.

Bridget went on. "Anyway, this is getting boring. I need to go home."

"Did you just take a selfie? Do not post anything with my officers in it. Are you driving back to Seattle? Is the address you gave me correct?"

"No. Mommy bought me a house next to her new beach house in Cabot's Cove."

"Of course, she did. Well, that's all I can tolerate and all we need."

Esther was just about to walk in the door when she felt a hand on her shoulder. She jumped and spun around to see her mother, arms crossed, a frown on her face.

"Esther James, what are you doing? I told you not to get involved," her mother hissed. "We had enough trouble. Your father's story was just on the front page of the paper a few days ago. Do you want to get me fired too?"

"I'm sorry, Mom. I was just coming to tell you we're going to the beach."

Waves of guilt and self-doubt washed through Esther, but she was silent. And then she felt it—the familiar drive to fight—anger, boiling up from deep inside.

"I know you like this young man a lot," her mother said, "and it's okay to support him, but how about from afar? Just until things settle down."

"Everyone needs support. Hart supported us when everything happened with Dad. What if Hart said it was none of his business?" Esther whispered.

Her mother's eyes grew huge and round. She cocked an eyebrow, and her lips became a firm line.

"You'd better tread lightly, little miss Esther. You are cruising for a grounding. I understand what you're saying, but I'm an adult and my life is none of your business."

"You married him. I don't even know what to call him. What if I make him as mad as I made Dad?" She folded her arms. The look in her mother's eyes was dark but also moist. Esther didn't want to hurt her, but her heart was pumping and everything she had been holding inside spilled over. "I don't need a new father. I'll be an adult soon. I need friends like Sophie and Parker, just like you need Hart. Parker needs us. Who else will be there for him if we aren't? What if his dad had something to do with their disappearance and Parker just can't see it?"

Her mother took a deep breath, let it out slowly, and seemed to think. She let Esther's words hang in the air for a minute and then said, "I know you feel like a grown-up, but don't rush to have grown-up responsibilities. I trust you, Esther. You're wise, and you have always made good decisions. That's why I don't understand this, except to say you have a crush on Parker. Don't do this for selfish reasons. Not now, when he's so vulnerable."

Esther couldn't believe what her mother was suggesting. The fighter in her took over. "I'm doing the right thing, and the right thing is to be there for my friend." She turned on her heels and walked away.

"Esther!" her mother said, loud enough to stop her.

Esther stopped and looked back at her.

"I love you. Be wise, okay?" Grace asked.

Esther nodded and kept walking.

After she rounded the corner of the house and was alone, she fell against the old shingle siding. Her heart was racing. *Why do I get so angry, so scared?* Her hands shook. She was trembling all over. She closed her eyes, and for a minute, just tried to slow her breathing. She flashed back in time to behind the couch. She wanted to save her mom. She should have saved her mom.

She didn't. But she could save Parker, and she was going to. He didn't have to live his life with regret. He didn't need to feel as alone as she did or as if it was all his fault.

"Pull it together," she said out loud and walked to the front yard and crossed the lawn heading toward her friends who were coming to meet her.

"What happened?" Nephi asked. "You look terrible."

"Thanks, jerk." She gave him a playful push. She still felt adrenaline coursing through her body. She put her hands into her hoodie pocket to hide the shaking. "I overheard the detective interviewing Bridget. She made it sound like Mr. Stuart did something to Paisley and her mom, but she doesn't know anything. She's just causing trouble."

The front door of the house opened, and they all stopped talking. Bridget came out, dressed in the same outfit she had worn to the party. She had a large black purse and big black sunglasses on. She walked across the lawn and toward a black hybrid car that looked sleek and new.

They watched her until she drove away.

"Come on," Nephi said. "Let's look on the beach where Paisley usually runs."

# 11

# Kids These Days

Hope drove and parked in the public lot at the cove near a massive piece of driftwood. They climbed over the rocks that littered the dune until they reached the soft sand of the beach. The tide was out, and the waterfront was empty except for a man playing fetch with his dog.

They hadn't walked far before Esther felt hopeless.

Nephi frowned. "The tide has been in already. What if it washed away any sign of her?" He stopped walking and scanned the horizon for signs of anything unusual. "I feel like praying."

Sophie's mouth fell open. "Who died and made you captain? I don't pray. What kind of God lets someone disappear? Huh?" Sophie asked. "Keep going." She motioned for them to follow her.

"God didn't make her disappear," Nephi retorted.

Sophie put her hands on her hips. "Listen, missionary, I'm a Christian too, I think. But right now, I am a girl detective. So, get detecting." Sophie picked up the pace and Esther tried to keep up.

*What kind of God?* The words hit her hard. She'd asked the same question a million times. She felt guilty for even thinking about it. She looked at Nephi and wasn't surprised to see that although he was walking through the sand, his eyes were closed. *He's praying.* Then he tripped over a piece of driftwood and they were all laughing again.

When she stopped to help him up, she saw Parker jogging to meet them and waved.

"Hey, guys!" Sophie shouted and began running the opposite way, back toward town. "Guys! Guys!" She bent over and picked something up off the beach.

Esther ignored Sophie and walked toward Parker. He looked awful. He rubbed his eyes but couldn't wipe away the sad look pulling down the corners.

"They're taking my dad to the police station. That detective is treating him like a suspect. I called his lawyer and brought him up to speed," Parker said between breaths.

"Guys!" Sophie was waving something as she ran toward them.

"Sophie, wait," Nephi said.

"What about you?" Nephi asked Parker.

Parker stood, still catching his breath. "They told me to wait. When they leave an officer will watch me. Someone from child welfare is supposed to come to the house."

"Child welfare?" Esther asked.

"You can't let them take you to foster care," Hope said.

Parker held up his pointer finger and they quieted. He finally caught his breath. "They won't." He smiled.

"What did you do?" Esther asked.

"We were in the study. The officer wanted to smoke. I told him I needed to go to the bathroom," he explained.

"Ah, the bathroom." Esther and Sophie laughed.

He bowed. "You guessed it. And then I left out the other door."

Nephi high-fived him. Without thinking, Esther gave Parker a hug.

"Guys!" Sophie shoved something into the circle. Esther looked at the wet thing in Sophie's hand, and her heart sank when she realized what it was.

Sophie held a wet dog collar and a short leash. A gold tag on the collar said "Cornwallis."

"Oh, no!" Parker took the collar gently and cleaned the sand off the gold tag with his thumb. "Oh, no . . . "

"I think this means we're on the right track." Nephi gently patted Parker on the shoulder. "She was out running and maybe the dog got away and she chased it."

Parker wasn't hearing him. Esther followed his gaze. He was searching the horizon, the ocean. She knew what he was thinking.

He had been here long enough to hear about sneaker waves—winter waves that washed farther than expected. He was wondering if she had been swept out to sea.

Nephi put his hand on Parker's shoulder. "We're going to find her. Besides, Paisley being caught in a wave doesn't explain where your mother is."

"You have a bigger problem," Hope said.

Parker turned and looked at her.

"What could be bigger than losing my mum and twin?"

"I'm sorry," she said softly. "If Child Protective Services are coming for you, they won't let you run around with a bunch of kids or help us look. They're going to want to talk to you. They might even take you someplace until this is all sorted out, like a foster home. The only good thing is this leash doesn't have to mean she's gone forever."

"My dad will be home soon. Besides, I can take care of myself." He frowned and folded his arms.

"I don't think they'll let you stay with him or be home alone." Hope shook her head. "Trust me. I know what I'm talking about. Foster kid, remember?"

"She does," Esther said.

"Should I go back?" Parker asked.

"Not yet. First we need to get everything we can from you, in case they place you in foster care and you can't call us," Hope explained.

"Okay. Let's keep looking for any sign of them while we talk." Parker raised his eyebrows and smiled.

"Let's finish scanning the beach," Esther said. When the tide comes in again, we'll lose any clues that are here."

"She's right," Parker said. "Let's walk down the beach while we talk until we reach the river. It will give us time to think."

"I don't know," Hope said. "What if she's alive and needs you? What can we do? We're just a bunch of kids. We need help! Maybe it's better if you go back and show them the leash. Then, you can let us know what the police have and what's happening until they decide whether to take you to foster care or not."

Esther looked past Parker at the churning surf. The thought of Paisley being in the water sent a shiver down Esther's spine. Her stomach churned. The northern Oregon ocean was so cold no one could survive very long without a wet suit.

"Guys!" Sophie said. "Don't give up. Think, Parker. Where else would they go? What do they do?"

Esther nodded. "Hope's right. We need to get some help. Let's call the police and have them meet us here so we can show them the leash."

"What can they do?" Parker asked.

Nephi pulled out his phone. "I don't know, but anything is better than nothing." He made the call. "Hello? This is Nephi, Grace's brother. Nephi. N-e-p-h-i. I know it's a different name. Hey, look. This is an emergency." He paused and rolled his eyes. "I called this number because it's where Hart works. No, I don't want to talk to him. I want to report an emergency." Totally frustrated, he put his hand on his hip.

"Okay," Nephi said. "Look, we were with Paisley. P-a-i-s- . . . "

"Give me that phone!" Sophie took the phone out of Nephi's hand.

Nephi tilted his head, "Hey!" He gave Sophie a look but let her keep the phone.

Sophie started talking loudly while pointing her finger, "Look, Paisley disappeared last night. Yes, it was—Listen! We just found her dog's leash in the surf." Esther could hear someone else talking on the other end. "I don't care what you think. The dog was with her when she went running and now the leash is in the ocean. You need to get someone out here to help find her . . . Good! At the cove. We can meet the officer at the cove by the water." Sophie hung up and slammed the phone into Nephi's open hand.

Parker's sad face was gone. He smiled. "I love it," he said and gave Sophie a gentle push.

"Sophie always gets it done." Esther grinned.

"Good job, Sophie," Hope said. "Now, Parker, tell us everything you know about Paisley, where she would go, and who she would call if she was upset."

"Well, she wouldn't run away," Parker offered.

The anguish on Parker's face made Esther's heart hurt. She couldn't just stand there without reaching out and putting a hand on his arm and moving closer. His eyebrows were knit as he struggled to maintain his composure. Taking a deep breath, he put his hand over hers.

"She's my twin, you know?" he said quietly. "I mean, she isn't perfect, but I can't stop feeling like she's in danger. I'm the older twin. We've always been there for each other, but . . . " His voice trailed off.

Something snapped deep in Esther's heart. "It will be okay," came out of her mouth before she even realized what she was saying. Immediately, her thoughts raced. *Is it? Is it really? It wasn't for me. How can I lie?*

"I know she's alive," he said. "We have a connection. You know?" He looked directly into her eyes, and she saw the moisture gathering in his. He glanced away and wiped his eyes with his arm, stood taller, and continued. "I thought she came back and went out with Bridget, but she obviously didn't. She doesn't go anywhere without her car. Her entire life is on social media."

"I've seen some of her posts. She takes a ton of selfies," Hope said. "We should look at her accounts. What if . . . " Parker's head snapped up, his eyes opened wide.

"Hey." Hope tucked a red curl behind her ear. She waited a moment and then said, "I didn't mean to say anything has happened. It's just, there are some bad people on social media." She stepped closer to him, looking into his eyes.

Esther watched Parker take his phone out and opened Paisley's social media. Over his shoulder, she saw a police car, lights off, parking at the cove.

An officer Esther didn't recognize picked his way down the rocks, slipped, and then called out as he walked toward them, "Are you Nephi?"

"I am," Nephi shouted. He waved at the officer.

The officer left the rocks below the cove parking lot and walked on the soft sand. When he got closer, Esther saw he had an animal control badge on and an orange vest over his uniform.

"Are you really an officer? We don't need a parking cop," Sophie said.

A laugh escaped Esther's lips. *Leave it to Sophie to say what I'm thinking.* She elbowed Sophie, who pushed back, their own friend code for 'way to go.'

"I am. I do animal control and parking too. But I am an official police officer." He adjusted the gear on his belt and proudly straightened his shoulders. "And you're Parker," he said. He turned to Parker, who took a step forward and offered his hand. The officer didn't take it. "I'm Officer Gustafson, and I'm supposed to take you back home."

"Wait!" Sophie stepped in front of Parker and put her hands out as if to stop the officer from snatching him and dragging him away. "You can't take him. We found his dog leash."

"Come again?" The officer chuckled and adjusted his hat.

Sophie kept talking, and no one was going to stop her. "His mom and sister are missing, and I just found their dog leash by the ocean. You have to search for them. Call the coast guard, search and rescue." Sophie pushed the leach into his face.

"I heard. That's why they sent me to take Parker back to the house," Officer Gustafson said. With one eyebrow cocked, he took the leash from Sophie and examined it. "Parker? Is this your dog's leash?"

"Yes, sir," Parker said.

"Where exactly did you find this?" The officer studied the leash in his hand.

Simultaneously they all pointed back to where Sophie found the leash on the beach.

The officer held up a finger and used the radio clipped to his shoulder and called dispatch, asking for a call from Detective Kohornen. Someone must have responded, although Esther couldn't hear the answer, because he had an earpiece. His phone rang, and he stepped away from the group to answer it.

He kept an eye on them while listening. He covered his mouth when he answered, so she only heard every other word. It sounded like he was explaining what they had found. Then he was studying Parker and their ragtag group.

"I see," the officer said. "Uh, huh. So she hasn't been gone long. Right." It went on for several minutes. Finally, he ended the call, pulled rubber gloves out of his pocket, and put them on. He set the leash down on a nearby piece of driftwood and, looking at Parker, asked, "Son, are you going to come with me peacefully?"

"I am happy to go with you." Parker held his hands up in the air in front of him while he talked like he was waiting for handcuffs. "But you have to promise to look for Paisley and my mother."

"Where are you taking him, really? Are you taking him to foster care?" Sophie stepped in front of Parker. The officer actually laughed.

"Hey, short stuff, let him go before I charge you with a felony for interfering with an officer. And you—too much TV. No cuffs," Gustafson said.

Sophie hung her head and turned around to face Parker and said, "Sorry, Parker, a felony would keep me from getting my financial aid, I think . . . " She shrugged.

Hope reached out and touched Parker's shoulder. "Don't worry. We'll look."

His shoulders relaxed. "Thanks, guys."

Parker walked in front of the officer back to the parking lot while they all watched in silence. The officer put him in the back of his car, with one hand on his head, closed the door, and left.

"Now what?" Nephi asked. "What are we supposed to do?"

"You keep looking," Hope said. "I have to go. I'm going to be late for work."

"Wait, you can't leave!" Sophie stood in front of Hope, hands on her hips, frowning.

"I don't want to, but I have to keep this job and I am already going to be late. Can you walk home or call Mable for a ride? You guys have got two of the smartest people I know standing right here. You can find her.

"Thanks," Nephi said. "We can walk home. It's not far."

"She didn't mean you." Sophie gave him a push. "But we need your muscle and charm. I've got an idea."

"Oh no," Esther groaned. "Please tell me we aren't going to do anything illegal."

Sophie grinned. "Just give me a minute." Sophie pulled out her phone and began working frantically.

Looking over Sophie's shoulder, Esther asked, "Are you cracking Paisley's password? What if she's fine? She'll kill you."

"She loves that dog. I'm betting her password is the dog and her birthday."

"No, it's her lucky number, seven," Nephi said. "You didn't hear that from me. When you go to jail, I'll be spending your financial aid."

"Fat chance. I'm going to say my name is Nephi if I get caught."

Esther found herself laughing while she watched Sophie try combinations. She pointed at the screen and said, "Try a dollar sign."

"Of course." Sophie raised her phone triumphantly. "We're in." She made sure the camera was turned away from her. She took a live video of the cove, and using a bizarre deep voice said, "We are in the Cove, at Necanicum, Oregon, where Paisley Pamela Stuart went missing last night. Listen, all you fans of Paisley, this is an S-O-S for your help. Just today we found her beloved dog's leash in the water. Paisley may be fighting for her life. We need your help. No matter where you are, no matter what you're doing, we need you to call the Necanicum Oregon Police Department and demand they search for Paisley. They think she ran away, but we know better. Paisley loves you all too much to leave you behind. Do your part. Call the Necanicum Oregon Police until they search for her. Oh, and use the non-emergency number." She stopped filming.

Nephi shouted, "Yes! Sophie, you're a genius. They have to look for her now! Woo-hoo!" He picked Sophie up and threw her in the air.

"Wait a minute, Moose! Put me down. I have to finish the post." She typed and talked out loud, while Nephi and Esther looked over her shoulder.

"Oh man, they're going to be so ticked," Esther said. "They should've listened." She couldn't help but laugh. Sophie was brilliant.

Sophie said what she was typing out loud as if they couldn't see it over her shoulder. "Don't just pray for her. Phone the police until they search. She is lost and this post is being put up by her friends. No one has seen her or her mother since last night. Help Paisley! Call the Necanicum Police at . . . what's their non-emergency phone number?"

Esther pulled out her phone, found it, and read it to Sophie.

"There. Now let's see if anyone is watching." Sophie held the phone and they stood in the sand looking at the number of likes and comments.

"Unbelievable," Nephi said. "I'm lucky if I get a few hundred likes."

"A few hundred?" Esther asked. "You get hundreds?"

"Everyone except you." He pushed her.

"Oh, guys, look!"

It was like watching a gas pump, the numbers were rolling so fast.

"We'd better get out of here," Esther said. "When people start calling, they're going to come see if the person that took the video's still here."

"Do you think they'll search now?" Nephi asked. "I mean, if they were going to search they would have sent out the town-wide text, called search and rescue, the coast guard. It would be obvious. I don't trust the detective. Do you think he is really going to do anything?"

"Who knows," Esther answered. "I want to go see what's happening with Parker."

"Look at you." Sophie half-smiled and shook her head as they walked back to the parking lot. "We broke the rules a few times today and you didn't die."

"The day is just getting started," Esther said.

"What are you talking about?" Nephi asked.

"Nothing," Esther said.

"Nothing," Sophie echoed and looked knowingly at Esther.

*She knows all of my secrets but one. The red couch day.*

Sophie's reminder of broken rules made her heart beat so fast she could feel it in her tight chest. *What else can we do? We're just kids . . .*

And then a thought skipped through her mind and landed straight in her heart: *You were only a kid.*

# 12

# It's for Your Own Good

Leaving the cove parking lot, they quickly walked and jogged toward Parker's house. Two police cars passed them. Then Esther's mother drove by.

Grace's car stopped. She opened her door, leaned out, and said something Esther couldn't quite hear.

"What did she say?" Nephi asked.

Esther went to her mother's car door.

"Hi, Mom," Esther said as brightly and cheerfully as she could manage.

"Esther! What are you doing? Go home!" Esther had never seen her mother's face look so frustrated. She was actually scowling.

"Okay."

"We are going to have a talk, young lady."

*Young lady?* "Okay, Mom. I just . . . "

"Now! Go home, now! You too Nephi," she yelled over Esther's shoulder. Nephi's eyebrows rose in shock. He pointed at himself like he was surprised and then shrugged like he didn't know what she was talking about. Esther groaned. She rubbed her forehead and eyes. Mom was going to kill them.

They stood on the sidewalk and watched Grace drive to the next block and parked. She got out and hurried to join the others inside Parker's house.

A blue sedan passed, and Esther's heart sank. "Guys! Guys!" She frantically ran back to the group.

"What was that?" Sophie asked.

"Move!" Esther said and pushed them ahead of her toward the tree house. "Let's go to the tree house. That's Karen!"

"Oh no!" Nephi sprinted.

Sophie passed him, and then, running easily, said over her shoulder to Esther, "Is anyone going to tell me who Karen is?"

"Mom's friend. Child welfare," was all Esther got out. Huffing and puffing from effort, she climbed the tree to get a bird's-eye view of the house, opened the trapdoor, and sprinted to the telescope. She turned it so she could see the window of the study. The door was still open partially.

"We have to get closer. You'll never hear up here." Nephi opened the trapdoor and climbed down. Sophie and Esther followed.

When they got to the corner of the house, they waited a minute while they caught their breath, and then gently tip-toed up onto the back porch, stopping with every squeak or sound their footsteps made.

They stood just outside the door and listened.

Parker's dad said, "It's only until we find your mom and sister. We'll get this all sorted out."

"Did they tell you about Cornwallis's leash?" Parker asked.

"What?" His father sounded surprised.

"His leash. Did they tell you we found it in the surf down on the beach?" Parker said.

"I don't understand."

"Listen, Mr. Stuart." Esther thought it was Detective Kohornen's voice. "The kids found the dog's leash on the beach, but we aren't sure what it means. There wasn't anything else visible."

"No. You listen, Detective. I want everyone possible out there searching for Paisley, or I will have my lawyer come after you!"

Esther smiled. Sophie threw both her arms in the air in a silent gesture of triumph.

"I'll make some calls," was all Kohornen offered.

"That's it? Make some calls? I'll look for her if you won't!" Parker shouted. Esther couldn't help herself. She leaned closer to the door and peeked in. She could see Parker standing. All the muscles in his back were tense, and he was clenching his fists. His father pulled him back down onto the couch.

Then the younger officer opened the living room door and brought Karen in to meet Parker. Her black hair fell over her face while she pulled a clipboard out of her large briefcase. She looked more like a librarian than a social worker. She adjusted her glasses and took a seat in a chair opposite Parker.

Detective Kohornen stood and said, "This is Karen, a child protective service worker."

"I'm not being abused." Parker leaned forward and his dad put his arm around him.

"It's all right, Parker. Detective Kohornen told me until we sort this out you need to stay with someone else."

Esther heard something behind her and turned to see Nephi walking quietly off the porch, phone in hand. Esther's eyebrows crinkled her forehead. Before she could call after him, he disappeared around the corner of the house.

The detective said, "I've been told we are going to call out search and rescue. I would like to get this taken care of. So let's get on with it."

Esther looked at Sophie, smiled, and winked. She motioned that they should follow Nephi. They carefully left the porch, taking the same silent steps they had before.

As soon as she rounded the corner she whispered to Nephi, "What are you doing?"

He still had his phone to one ear. He put his finger to his lips, telling her to be quiet.

"Uh, huh. He can have mine. It's okay. Thanks." He hung up.

"What was that?" Sophie asked.

"A long shot," Nephi said. "Follow me."

He headed around the front of the house and started up the stairs.

"Uh, no way, cowboy!" Sophie said. "Are you trying to get Esther grounded for the rest of her life?" Esther nodded in agreement.

"Okay, you'd better wait here." He didn't wait for their answer. He opened the front door and walked into the house like he owned it.

Sophie looked at Esther, both their eyes wide and their mouths opened. They practically tripped over each other running back around the house and to the study door.

They could hear Esther's mom apologizing, then Nephi's deep voice, then the detective, Parker, and Mr. Stuart.

"That's the perfect plan. Nephi is a nice young man. I've met his family at track meets. I approve," Mr. Stuart said loudly.

"I would have to get approval," Karen said. Before she could finish her sentence her phone played an Irish jig. "Hello? Yes? Oh. I see. But . . . . Right. Thanks." She hung up.

Everyone stared at the child protective service worker. She held all the power over Parker's life. Esther felt something brush her leg and jumped. It was Sophie, down on all fours, trying to see into the room.

"Parker, I have authorization to leave you in the custody of your friend Nephi's mother, Mable. She is a certified foster parent. If your father approves. You are to have your own room. You are not to share a room with Nephi or with Hope. Get your things."

"Wait a minute," Esther's mom said.

"Do you have a problem with the arrangement, Grace?" Karen asked.

Esther's mom looked at Parker's father, who shook his head no.

"Okay then, Parker, let's go to Mable's house." Karen gathered her things.

"Yes!" Esther hissed and clapped her hand over her mouth. Sophie silently laughed and Esther raised her fists in the air in triumph. They scrambled back across the porch and ran for the nearby cove.

# 13

# Be My Guest

"Parker's going to stay at your house!"

"I know! I have to clean my room! Hurry," Esther shouted.

"What about Paisley?" Sophie asked.

"Oh." Esther stopped dead in her tracks. "You're right. We need to go home, get Parker, and get back out to the cove and walk the beach to see if we can find any more clues or find someone who saw them. I'm going to text Hope and let her know what's happening."

"Hey, wait!" Nephi waved and called to them from the porch. He easily jogged to their side.

Esther smacked herself in the forehead. "Hope has the SUV! She drove it to work."

"Well, I guess we're walking," Nephi said.

"Let's take the beach. That way we can look for more clues," Esther said. "Besides, it's faster."

"Great. Then I can tell a six-foot-four-inch, two-hundred and twenty-pound cop, and my new brother-in-law, I invited one more person to stay with us. Are they allowed to use their taser off duty?"

"Don't worry. I always protect my future company's employees, dork boy. I'm going to need a chauffeur when I'm rich." Sophie slugged him in the arm.

When they rounded the corner and were on the last block before the cove, they all stopped and stared.

"It worked!" Esther gave Sophie a high-five with the entire friend slap and smack dance. Nephi just stood with his mouth open.

The cove was full of cars, and twenty or thirty high schoolers stood in groups around the police chief. A search and rescue vehicle was trying to park, and an officer with a dog tugging on the leash was holding the dog back.

And Roger Abbott was filming the whole thing for the news.

The chief climbed on top of a picnic table and raised his hands to silence everyone. No one paid any attention at first. He shouted, "Listen Up! I don't know who told you to call us, but it has to stop! We can't even conduct business as usual!"

Alfred, a local senior in high school, yelled back, "What are you doing to find Paisley?"

"We want Paisley. We want Paisley!" the crowd started chanting.

One of the search and rescue team members from the county sheriff's department handed the chief a bullhorn.

He turned it on and tested it. "Alfred, go home."

"You can't make me! We want Paisley. We want Paisley." Alfred climbed on a log, pulled up his baggy pants, and raised his arm, pumping his fist and leading the chanting.

The chief took out his phone and texted someone. He raised the bullhorn. "I just texted your dad, Al. He says you're wanted at home."

Alfred's eyes got as big as Coke bottle bottoms. He scrambled off the log, while the crowd laughed and headed down the road toward town. The crowd kept chanting.

"Quiet down! We are closing the beach so the search and rescue dog can do its job," the chief said through the bullhorn.

"Let us help!" Sophie shouted.

"Sophie. Knock it off," Esther said. "If I get in any more trouble, I won't be able to go to college because I'll be grounded until I'm thirty."

"Anyone who doesn't comply will be charged with interfering with our investigation. If you want to help Paisley, and you have real and useful information, then you can see the officer over there." The chief pointed at an officer who didn't appear to be paying attention.

The officer's head popped up and his mouth fell open. He looked back and forth and then began backing up until he was against his vehicle, surrounded by angry teenage boys.

Esther and Sophie retreated, watching the crowd disperse.

"Look." Sophie pointed at Mr. Stuart, Parker's father, making his way through the crowd to the search and rescue team.

"Let's go tell Parker," Nephi said.

# 14

# Shih Tzus! You Won't Regret Practicing

By the time they walked to Esther and Nephi's house, Sophie's mother had called her three times.

"I have to go to feed the Shih Tzu and practice for violin lessons. I'll be back." Sophie peeled off and ran toward her house, just down the road from Esther's.

"Let's hope Grace doesn't yell as loud with Parker in the room," Nephi said. They both stopped at the bottom of the stairs and looked at the front door with dread. They watched Karen walk to her state sedan and drive away. Esther wanted to cheer.

When a cloud covered the sun, they looked up at the sky just in time to feel heavy raindrops fall on their faces.

"I guess we better go in," Nephi said.

"I'm okay waiting. Besides, you're used to getting in trouble."

Nephi gave Esther a friendly shove and a half smile. They walked in sync, step by step.

As if she felt them coming, her mother opened the screen door. Esther's mom was silent. She stepped aside, held the door open, and pointed into the living room. Her lips were pressed together, and her eyes were like lasers, forcing them both to look at the floor.

Hart stood silently next to her, holding a large mixing bowl and spoon. He was wearing an apron. Mable stood by the fireplace.

Esther's seven-year-old sister, Mary, was rocking the chair by the fire as hard as she could, chanting, "You're in trouble, you're in trouble."

"Esther, I know your worried . . . " Hart started to say. Esther's eyes narrowed, her lips pressed together. *I don't want any advice from my mom's husband.* A beeping from the kitchen interrupted them.

Hart headed for the kitchen. Smoke was rolling out of the oven.

"Mary, knock it off," Nephi said. She stuck her tongue out at him.

"Mary!" Esther's mom said.

"Nephi," Mable said.

Nephi looked back down like a whipped puppy.

"Sorry, dude," Parker offered from the couch.

Esther was so lost in her own shame, she hadn't realized Parker was in the room. And now, Parker was going to witness the entire thing.

Grace turned to Esther and asked, "Do you want to explain to Grandma Mable why I am not sure having Parker stay with her as her foster son is a good idea? That when Parker's around you all lose your minds? That today you were told not to go to Parker's multiple times and went anyway?" Grace's voice got higher as she said, "Tell her how you put yourselves in jeopardy, not to mention my job?" Grace folded her arms when she finished talking. She looked at Mable, her mouth in a firm line. Mable shrugged.

Esther felt like throwing up. Her knees were weak, and she wanted to disappear into the floor.

Just then, the door opened, and Sophie came in already talking. "I would have been faster, but I couldn't find the dog's bib and had to heat her food."

She stopped short when she felt the thick tension in the room. "Whoa. I didn't know you got mad, Mrs. James. Or is it Mrs. Hart now?"

Her mother's color rose until she boiled over. "That's because Esther's never done anything like this before—in her life. What kind of friends would encourage her to get into this much trouble?"

"It's my fault, Mrs. Hart," Parker said, standing.

Esther's head snapped up. She was trembling and nauseated, but Parker stood tall, beautiful, and although exhausted, calm.

"I was afraid for my mum and Paisley. I didn't think." Then his voice broke. He looked down, one hand resting on his hip while the other covered his eyes for just a minute. His chest heaved. After a moment he composed himself and said, "I apologize. I won't do it again."

Esther had never seen a boy or even a man be so brave and open. She looked from him to her mother, who was obviously melting. Her mom's shoulders dropped, and her hands fell to her side.

Grace crossed the room and became the mother Esther recognized when she gathered Parker in a hug and held him while he went from a strong man to a little boy with shaking shoulders and silent tears, a boy who just wanted his mother. And yet, Esther felt more respect for him than any man she had ever met.

"I'm sorry too, Parker," Grace said. "I am just climbing out of a mess with Esther's father, and . . . " She stopped herself. "It doesn't matter. All that matters now is finding your mom and sister. We can clean the rest of this up later."

At that moment, an enormous roar vibrated the house as it flew over it. Sophie ran out on the porch. Everyone followed her and searched the sky.

"It's the channel eight news copter!" Sophie pointed at it in the southern sky, hovering over the trees and moving toward the cove.

"Good grief," Mable said. "Who organized the party, Sophie?"

Sophie grinned. No shame at all. Esther wanted to be Sophie more than anyone on earth, or Parker, who seemed to bravely do the right thing without question.

*A news helicopter? I hope we did the right thing.* She scanned her family's faces as they watched the sky. *They all look like it's a triumph. What if they find Paisley and her mom washed up on the rocks?* She looked at Parker's hopeful face while he stood on the porch with her family, watching the helicopter circle the beach. The familiar feeling of anxiety rose from deep inside.

A hand touched her, bringing her back into the present. It was Parker. He smiled at her. Although she was still anxious, a thought traveled through her mind. *Stay here, now. You're safe.*

Even though she didn't know where the thought came from, she liked it. *I'm safe,* she told herself.

"Wait a minute," Sophie said. "Wait just a minute. How did they get here so fast? Portland is two hours away. Even by helicopter it seems fast. Something must have happened. Do you think the local newspaper or Roger Abbott called the Portland news station?"

Grandma Mable cackled. She had a strange twinkle in her eye.

"What's going on, Mom?" Nephi asked.

"Maybe Sophie isn't the only one making calls," Mable said.

"Mom!" Grace said.

"Wait a minute." Sophie's eyes narrowed. She folded her arms and studied Grace. "Did you call the news, Mom James? Or is it Mom Hart now?"

"No. And even if I did, I couldn't tell you," Grace replied.

"You called someone . . . " Sophie let the last word trail off.

"Hm." Grace raised her eyebrows and motioned like she was locking her lips and throwing away the key. She marched off the porch and back into the house, letting the screen door slam behind her.

Then Grace peeked back out the door at Parker. "If I were you, I would look for my sister and mother." The screen slammed again.

"Oh my gosh," Parker said, laughing. "Your mother is the best." He looked down at Esther, who was smiling.

"My mother doesn't break the rules," Esther said. "I'm sure whatever she did was perfectly fine."

"Your mother may not break the rules," Grandma Mable snickered. "But she understands them so well, she can almost always find a way to work around the rules. She gave me Karen at Child Welfare's cell number and Karen's supervisor's number so I could text them and offer to keep Parker here. Because I have Hope, I became a certified foster parent. I think Karen's supervisor was grateful to have a safe place for him to go so quickly. I texted them earlier today. And, Esther, your mom trusted you. That's why she was so upset when you didn't do what she told you to. Remember who you are and make good choices." And with that, she joined Grace inside.

Esther could hear her mother inside the house. "Mom! You should tell them . . . " Then the conversation became muffled. For a split second, Esther wondered if her mom would get into trouble at work for whatever it was she had done to get help for Parker and his dad.

Worried that they might get into one of their louder discussions, she took Parker by the hand.

"Let's go see what's going on," Esther said.

"We better tell your mum that we're going," Parker said.

"I will." Nephi poked his head inside the door and called, "Grace! Mom! We're going to the cove to see what's going on. I have my cell phone. Okay."

"What did she say?" Esther asked.

"They were still talking. She just waved." Nephi took the stairs two at a time. They followed him across the street.

"Hey!" Hart was yelling at them from the front porch. "Where's my SUV?" Sophie ran even faster.

"Hope has it at work! " Nephi yelled back at Hart. He caught up with Sophie.

Esther raised her eyebrows and shook her head. "Do you think this time we can stay out of trouble? Please." He just smiled, shrugged, and kept pace with her.

# 15

# You'll Understand When You're Older

When they were close to the center of town, they left the beach and gathered on the sidewalk on top of the broad sea wall. The sea wall rose several feet above the beach and kept the ocean from washing sand into town during winter tides. The sky was gray. A light fog had blown in, reducing visibility. The cool air felt good.

"I need to go to the Soup, Smoothie & Tea and get the keys from Hope," Nephi said.

"I'll come with you," Sophie replied.

"Esther and I will keep going. Somehow, I'm sure you two can catch up and pass us." Parker winked at Nephi.

Esther studied his face and thought, *When this is over, could he ever like me?*

Parker looked at Esther, narrowed his eyes, and asked, "Is that all right? You look like you're not sure."

"Of course," she said.

*He reads me like an open book,* Esther thought, alarmed. The only other person who saw through her was Sophie. *He won't like me if he knows what a mess I am.*

Part of her wanted to be around him and couldn't stop thinking about him. Another part of her knew he couldn't possibly love her. *I should just push him away and get it over with,* she thought.

Parker jogged easily alongside her. "Hey, are you okay going alone, just us?"

"Sure," she said, trying to sound more relaxed than she was.

He slowed to a walk and took her hand to hold her back. "I thought it might give us some time to talk. We haven't had many chances to chat, other than the bookstore and tree house."

She slowed to a walk and realized he wasn't letting go of her hand.

"Are you worried?" she asked.

His face clouded over and he looked down. He bit his lip and then picked up their walking pace.

"I'm sorry," she said. "I shouldn't have asked."

He squeezed her hand harder and said, "I can't let myself go there. I feel Paisley is in trouble, and I'm sure they are together. The thought won't leave me. I want to throw up. I can't breathe when I think about it. I felt so totally helpless this morning."

She just listened and let him talk.

"Somehow, I feel like Mum is okay. I don't know why. It's just a feeling." He was silent for a minute.

She wanted to say something brilliant, something that would make it all okay. She didn't know what to say, so she said what she had wanted to hear all those years ago, when her own life was unraveling.

"It isn't your fault."

He stopped walking without warning and picked her up in a tight and wonderful hug. She couldn't help it; she leaned into him and hugged him back.

"You always know the right thing to say," he said into her ear. "I have been blaming myself for not running with her ever since I realized she was gone." His voice broke. He pulled away and began walking again. Reaching back he held his hand open and waited until she put her hand in his.

"I keep thinking I haven't been a very good brother lately. If I had been there for her, instead of being annoyed at her, she would have talked to me instead of going running in the dark alone, like a stupid idiot. I should have stopped her, or at least tried to talk to her."

"I don't know if I'd listen to Nephi if he tried to stop me," Esther offered.

"It isn't the same. Not to say that doesn't matter. It's just, well, we're twins. There is something I can't explain to our twinness, a connection."

Embarrassed and thinking she had said the wrong things, she remained silent.

Finally, he said to her, "Have you ever done anything you regret?"

"Yes." The red couch flashed in her mind and she felt herself break out in a sweat.

"What happened?" he asked.

She remained silent, even though part of her wanted to tell him everything, all of it. She felt like she could trust him. He was kind and strong. But what if that was just an act?

"Please." He stopped walking again to look at her. He reached out and touched her cheek. "You're helping me. I know things have been hard, because Nephi and I are friends, and well, I saw the post Abbott did on social media. Honestly, that's why I thought you and Nephi would understand."

"I wish I did," Esther said. "I'm so worried about Paisley and your mom. I can't imagine how you must feel."

"I feel like my world is coming unraveled and nothing is working out yet. I read what your dad did. What if my mom left and took Paisley with her? I can't imagine she would, but what if? I know it isn't the same as your dad, but why would he try to take you from your mom if he loves you? I mean, why would my mom take Paisley from us? Your father must have loved you. How could he not?"

*He must have loved me.* Her mother had said the same thing. But how could love motivate something so awful?

"Have you let someone down before?" Parker asked. "Like you failed them miserably and you'd do anything to fix it?" He locked eyes with her and waited for what felt like forever and said, "I know, I've met your mom. Your life with your mom is probably perfect."

"Perfect? Are you kidding me?" They both walked and the flood gate opened. She couldn't stop herself. "Perfect? First of all, have you really met my mother? She is always coming and going. I talk to Grandma Mable more. I mean, she's great, but I screwed up our entire family! My mom and dad were having a fight like your mom and dad, and not only did I not step in, I caused it! I wouldn't stop whining and crying. I was really little, but I can still remember it like it was yesterday.

"I was standing behind a red couch crying. No, I was . . . " A memory flashed before her eyes. She was on a rug with blocks, and they had all fallen after she had worked hard on stacking them. She started crying. "I was throwing a fit because my blocks fell, and my mother put me behind the couch. She told me to be quiet."

Suddenly, Esther realized something she had never understood before. "She threw me behind the red couch to keep me safe. She stood between me and him to protect me."

They walked in silence for several seconds, while Esther was lost in thought.

"Is that why your father was in prison?" Parker asked. "I don't understand what you did wrong."

"No. Yes." She had kept everything a secret for so long. It had never come out of her mouth. She didn't know how to say it. "Well, he went to prison, because my mother was pregnant and he tried to kill her . . . and the baby, my little sister, Mary."

All of a sudden she was in Parker's embrace. "I am so sorry," he whispered.

She should have been sobbing, but she wasn't. She felt like a weight had just lifted off her chest. Something about saying it out loud brought it all back, but she saw it differently, like a grown-up.

"I was a child, Parker." She gently pulled herself back from him, so she could see his eyes. "I was just a little girl, and I blamed myself, thinking I should have stopped him. I should have gotten between him and my mother, when he was an adult, with a weapon."

"It wasn't your fault," he said.

"And it isn't yours." She looked in his eyes. He was far away, thinking, looking somewhere off in the distance. "Paisley knows you love her. She would have come to you if she needed you."

"If she doesn't now, when I find her, she will know I love her," he said. "Come on, let's get to the cove. Only a few more blocks.

# 16

# Going off the Deep End

Esther couldn't believe the chaos at the cove. Just as they made it to the nearest cross street a news van with a channel four logo on the side pulled up. The news helicopter in the sky had left, but the search and rescue vehicle was still in the parking lot. The police had put up police tape and cones. They were directing traffic away from the area, but they let the van through after what looked like a brief exchange of words after the driver flashed a press badge.

"Hey, guys! Wait!" Sophie sprinted easily in their direction. Nephi was close on her heels, red faced, and trying to keep up. She was waving a brown bag.

"I got us a whole bag of bagels!" Sophie shouted triumphantly.

They got as close as they could to the search and rescue vehicle, trying not to draw attention to themselves.

"Nephi, look shorter," Sophie said. "The chief is going to see you and call Grandma Mable to come get you."

"I have an excuse. I'll tell him we're here to get my vehicle, or Hart's anyway." Nephi smirked.

"Seriously," Esther said. "We are all going to need to repent after this."

Nephi gave her a friendly shove, and Parker smiled. He whispered in her ear, "Don't be too hard on us."

She shook her head. "My standards have dropped like a bomb."

"Thank you for deeming us worthy, your highness," Nephi said.

"You're lucky we always let the court jester tag along," Sophie retorted.

Esther watched the news van. "What do you suppose they're doing?"

"Hopefully, they will put out a press release asking for help to find them," Parker said. "Look." He pointed down the beach.

The entire beach was empty. Police and signs stood ready to keep everyone off. It looked like deputies from the search and rescue team had lined up the width of the beach. Every once in a while they would take a step forward. They had rakes and were sifting through the sand, looking for any clue that might lead them to Paisley.

All the phones in the crowd of people around them suddenly made an odd sound. The entire crowd pulled their phone out of their pockets or purses and looked.

"It's an Amber Alert! Perfect," Sophie said.

"Sophie," Parker said, "I can't thank you enough. None of this would have happened if it wasn't for you."

"Yeah, well, you can thank me when we find her alive and well," Sophie said.

Esther had rarely seen her this serious. "Sophie, you should be a detective. You would do a better job than Kohornen."

"Duh," was all Sophie said.

"Hey," Nephi said, "it looks like they're going to do something. The crews have the cameras out. Parker, you should go talk to them about Paisley and your mom. Maybe you can tell them something that will help, like what they look like."

"I think you're right." Parker tried to smooth his hair by taking it out of the ponytail holder and putting the ponytail back in.

"Good grief," Sophie said. "Even when you're a slovenly mess, you look like a male model!"

"Soph!" Esther couldn't help it. She smiled.

"Thanks." He took a deep breath, and they started doing the impossible, moving in a crowd toward the news crew.

"What's going on?" Sophie asked. She jumped to try to see over the top of the people surrounding her.

"Sophie, be careful." Nephi put his arm out and tried to protect her short frame as they moved toward the news camera.

Parker held Esther's hand, but when they got close, he let go and moved toward the reporters.

As he got closer, Roger Abbott, the local reporter, stepped in front of him, halting his progress. He shoved his small microphone into Parker's face.

"Roger Abbott, Coho County News. Can you tell me why your sister ran away?"

"She didn't," Parker snapped. His face turned red.

Abbott didn't let up. "Has your father been arrested for abusing your mother before?"

Nephi leapt in front of Esther and grabbed Parker by the shoulders and held him back. Parker spun around, his nostrils flared, his hands in fists. "Let go."

"No, man. Don't let him get to you," Nephi said.

Parker closed his eyes, breathing hard.

Abbott smirked.

Before Esther could move, Sophie passed her and pushed Abbott back. "He said get out of his way!"

Abbott threw his arms up in the air. "Whoa, Officer! Help! I'm being assaulted."

The crowd backed up, forming a circle around Abbot and their group. Officer Ironpot joined them in the circle.

"Calm down! Calm down!" Ironpot repeated until the crowd quieted. For just a moment the cove was almost silent except for the wind.

"Now," Ironpot asked, "what's wrong, Abbott?"

"Sure, ask the grown-up! Don't listen to the youth!" Sophie barked at Ironpot.

"Simmer down, Sonoko. Is your mother here?" Ironpot scanned the crowd.

"She assaulted me," Abbott said. He got in Ironpot's face and said, "I want her arrested."

"This little girl?" Ironpot asked. He looked Sophie's four-foot-eleven frame up and down. "I don't think she's even ninety pounds. What do you weigh, Abbott?" The crowd laughed.

"She pushed me!"

The crowd laughed again.

"Are you injured?" Ironpot asked in a very serious tone.

"Not yet. Let me try again," Sophie said.

"All right, Sophie, move along." Ironpot led her out of the circle. He stopped, while still holding her arm, leaned into her face, and asked, "What are you doing here? Do your parents know you're here?"

"Yes. She's with me." Parker stepped up to address Ironpot. "We were trying to get to the other reporters before Abbot stopped us.

"Are you sure you want to talk to them?" Ironpot asked him.

Parker nodded.

"Does Mable know you're here?"

Nephi moved in closer to Ironpot and said, "They know we're here."

"And I am sure she won't mind if I talk to the news," Parker added.

"Don't you want to ask your dad first?" Ironpot asked. "He's over in the search and rescue vehicle. We're trying to keep the crowd away from him."

Parker nodded and Ironpot, with his hand on Parker's back, began guiding him toward the search and rescue truck.

"Make way," Ironpot said to anyone who wasn't paying attention.

Esther saw the newscaster step in front of their small camera. He held a microphone and began pointing at the search and rescue workers, explaining what was going on.

The reporter motioned for a girl to come closer. Rachel, a girl from Esther's school, joined him. They were finally close enough now and could hear what was said.

Esther reached out and touched Ironpot's back to get his attention. He stopped Parker and waited to see what she wanted.

"Look!" Esther pointed at the girl by the reporter.

"Who's that?" Parker asked.

"This is Jack Jones reporting for channel four news. I'm here with Rachel, a friend of Paisley's and fellow student at Oceanside High. Rachel, what do you know about Paisley's disappearance?"

"Paisley and I are best friends. Paisley, if you hear this, come home! We all saw Bridget's post and we won't let your dad treat you like that! We're here for you, girlfriend." Rachel wiped a tear that Esther couldn't see.

"Thank you, Rachel. This is Jack Jones hoping Paisley Stuart responds to her best friend's plea. Come home, Paisley."

The cameraman motioned to Jack, who said, “That’s a wrap. Thanks, Rachel.”

“What time will I be on the air?” Rachel asked while reapplying her lipstick.

“That was live.”

Several girls from Oceanside High began giggling and visibly fawning over Rachel when she joined them.

“Who is that?” Parker asked.

“Isn’t that your sister’s best friend?” Ironpot asked with a half-smile on his face.

“No, mate. I’ve never seen her before. Even in school.”

“They all come out when the moon’s full,” Ironpot said.

Parker looked up. Ironpot shook his head and added, “It’s just an expression.”

“She’s crazy,” Sophie said, helping Parker understand what Ironpot was trying to say. “Let’s go see your dad.”

Parker quickly closed the distance to the truck. His dad was sitting in the passenger seat. He was wearing a baseball cap, and his eyes looked tired. When he turned to look at Parker, Esther could see the scratches on his cheek were healing, but a new bruise was emerging just under the black circles around his eyes. He lit up when he saw Parker.

He pushed the door open and pulled Parker into a tight embrace. Esther watched the love between father and son and for a split second had a pang of jealousy. But then she thought, *Every father should love their children like that.* Warmth spread from her heart all the way to her toes, like loving confirmation of her thoughts.

“I am so sorry,” Mr. Stuart said quietly.

“It’s not your fault, Dad. I don’t know what happened, but don’t blame yourself.”

“When did you get so wise?” his father asked.

Parker smiled and said, “I know. I blame myself too. I can’t stop thinking about it all . . . ”

Then Parker reached out for Esther and pointed at the group of friends.

“You remember, Esther, Nephi, and Sophie?” Parker said to his father as he opened the embrace and looked back for them.

"Thank you for taking care of Parker," he said to Nephi.

"Anytime. He's one of us now." Color spread from Nephi's neck to his face.

Esther couldn't remember ever seeing Nephi this humble.

"Enough of this reunion. Have they found anything?" Sophie asked.

Mr. Stuart actually smiled and chuckled softly. "No. Well, not that they've told me."

"Who's in charge of this circus? Seriously? Why isn't the coast guard out there in their helicopter?" Sophie pointed out at sea.

"Do they do that?" Mr. Stuart asked.

"Man, you are new to town. We have a high angle rescue team, the coast guard rescue swimmers, we got it all! Have they brought in a dog?"

"Yes, but they said the dog couldn't find a scent on the beach." Mr. Stuart watched the searchers. "At least the rain stopped."

"Dad, I really want to talk to the news crews. I want to ask for help from everyone to find Paisley and Mum."

Parker's father nodded. "I've been avoiding them. My attorney said not to talk to anyone, but it's time to put all that aside and just find them." He put a protective arm around Parker's shoulder and said, "Let's go. All we can do is our best."

While Mr. Stuart pushed through the crowd toward the news crews, Esther, Sophie, and Nephi followed. The crowd started pushing back and a murmur rippled through it, like broken sentences in the wind. Then they recognized Parker's father.

"It's him! He's the one!" some large boy in a red coat yelled. "Look! Look! It's Paisley's father, the one that killed her!"

Esther's heart almost stopped. She knew Parker's father was a suspect, but to hear it said out loud filled her with doubt. *What if he did kill her?*

She grabbed Sophie and pulled her half a step back, while the crowds continued yelling at them.

"What if he did?" Esther asked.

Sophie looked at her like she was crazy. "Look at him! Look at how Parker looks at him. What do you think?"

"My gut says no," she said.

"Why don't you trust yourself? You're almost as smart as me, and I'm your future valedictorian." Sophie smiled. She loved pointing out that she was going to be the class valedictorian.

"You're right," Esther said. Even if she couldn't trust her own judgment of men, she trusted Sophie. She shook off her worries and watched as Parker and her father got closer to the news crew.

The police chief was also pushing his way through the crowd toward them.

"Mr. Stuart!" he called. "Rob!"

Parker's father stopped when he heard his first name and waited for the chief to reach him. The crowd clued in, quieted, and watched the conversation.

The chief got close enough to talk in a normal tone, which was easy while everyone looked on silently.

"Mr. Stuart," he repeated. "You know everything you say to that camera will follow you into a courtroom?"

"That's what my attorney told me, but it's time to put all that aside and do whatever I can for my family." With that, Parker's father took the last few steps toward the reporter, whose cameraman was filming all of it.

"Mr. Stuart, Jack Jones, channel four news. Can we ask you a few questions?"

"Yes, and then my son and I would like to make a statement."

"This is your son, Paisley's brother?" the reporter asked.

Esther noticed the chief turn on a small recorder and hold it out to the group, recording every word they said.

"My name is Parker, Parker Stuart, and I'm Paisley's twin," Parker said. His father stood next to him, arm still around his shoulder. Esther watched fascinated by the look of love on his father's face.

She had never had a father to love her like that. *What would it be like*? she wondered again.

Jack Jones pulled the mic from Parker back to himself and said, "Tell us, Parker, how do you feel?"

Parker's left eyebrow rose, just slightly, letting Esther know he thought this was a stupid question. "I'm here to ask for the public's help. Paisley wouldn't run away, and neither would my mother. They simply wouldn't leave without telling us. All of her friends and fans on

YouTube and social media believe she's a happy person. This isn't like her. Something has happened to her. If you know anything, anything at all, please contact . . . " And then he looked blank for a second.

The chief put the recorder down and stepped in front of the microphone. "You can contact the Necanicum Police Department." After he gave the number he paused. "We will set up a tip line. Watch for more on our social media pages."

"Chief believes Parker." Sophie smiled victoriously.

Jack Jones took the mic back. "Mr. Stuart, do you have anything to add? Do you think your wife and daughter ran away? We've been told you argued last night after a party at your house."

Mr. Stuart ignored the reporter's jab, took the mic, and said, "Melissa, Paisley." His voice broke. He took a deep breath, stood up taller, and went on. "I love you. We need you. If you are out there, please come home. And if someone has you, we will not stop until we find you." Then a thought crossed his face. His eyes narrowed, and he balled his fists and stood taller. "And if anyone out there has hurt my beloved Melissa or my baby girl, I'm coming for you."

Fear jolted through Esther. *What if I'm wrong? What if he's just like my dad? All that anger.*

"Wow," Sophie said. "I want him to be my dad!" She raised her tiny fist and yelled, "Yeah!" The crowd shouted their approval.

"Sophie!" Esther scolded. "Doesn't his anger scare you?"

"Anger? That man is terrified." Sophie shook her head. "What I wouldn't give for a father that protective. The worst mine could do is spill ink on you, criticize your pocket protector, or comment on your DNA strands."

"I bet he could invent an awesome laser gun." Nephi elbowed Sophie. His buddy-gesture knocked her off her feet. She stumbled into Esther.

"Dude!" she said.

Jones looked straight at the camera, "This is Jack Jones reporting for channel four. You heard it here first. Mr. Stuart would like his wife and daughter returned. Should she come home? What if home is the most dangerous place of all?"

Mr. Stuart's shoulders fell. He shook his head and patted Parker on the back.

"Good grief," Nephi said, loud enough for Jack to hear.

"Out of my way, Paul Bunyan," the reporter said. He pushed past Nephi. The cameraman followed.

"Rob! Rob!" Esther heard a woman's desperate shouts and looked to see where they were coming from.

A Black Range Rover was stopped at the police tape on the road. Melissa Hearst-Stuart, Parker's mother, had opened the passenger door and was hanging out of the car waving frantically.

"Rob!" she screamed at her husband over the noise of the crowd.

As if they had a collective mind, the mob realized what was going on. Confused, they cleared a path for her. The police moved the tape and let the Range Rover through.

"Madison." Sophie pointed at the car.

"Madison?" Esther asked. She followed Sophie's finger. Madison Merriweather, the author, was driving the Range Rover. Melissa, Parker's mother, was leaning out the passenger window. She had on black sunglasses, so it was hard to see her expression, but she was waving both arms at her husband.

Mr. Stuart started pushing his way through the crowd, Parker on his heels.

"Come on!" Sophie said and grabbed Esther's hand, pulling her along behind them, Nephi right behind them.

When the car came to a stop, Parker's mother jumped out of the SUV and fell into her husband's arms. Parker put his arms around both of them.

"Where's Paisley?" Parker asked.

"She isn't with me," his mother said. She took her sunglasses off, tipped her head, and looked into her husband's eyes.

"We've been searching for you both. No one has seen her since last night," Mr. Stuart said. Parker's mom put her hand over her mouth, her eyes wide. Mr. Stuart looked down, took her hand, and pulled her closer to him.

Jack Jones pushed Esther out of the way and stood by Parker. He said to the cameraman, "Go live, go live!"

The cameraman pointed at the reporter and Jack said, "You saw it here first, folks! Melissa! Melissa! Channel four news! Where have you been, Mrs. Stuart! Care to comment for the public?

Esther's heart caught in her throat as she realized Parker's mom was sobbing and clinging to her husband. How could people who had had a violent fight love each other so much? She was so confused.

Mr. Stuart was crying and talking quietly to his wife. Esther couldn't hear anything over the chaos. Then she saw Parker's lips move, catching snippets. She realized he was saying, "I love you."

The crow quieted and Esther heard Parker's mother say, "I love you too. I'm so sorry. I'm so sorry," she said over and over again. "I'm terrified for Paisley. I just wanted a night off, a break. I didn't mean to scare you."

"I'm sorry," Parker's dad said.

"No. I'm the one who should be sorry. I was totally out of line. I'm so sorry we fought. If I hadn't been so awful, none of this would have happened. It's all my fault." Mrs. Stuart buried her head in his shoulder, and he whispered something Esther couldn't hear, patting her back and comforting her.

Esther watched in fascination as she witnessed something she had never seen in a marriage; forgiveness.

The reporter shoved his hand and mic in their faces. "Mrs. Stuart, where were you?" he bellowed.

The chief had had enough, and he put his hand on the reporter's shoulder and firmly said, "Step away, son. If they want to talk to you, I'll let you know."

"I'll talk to you," said an arrogant voice behind Esther. She turned to see Madison Merriweather and Bridget, standing side by side, towering over her in platform shoes, made up like they had just left a New York beauty salon, camera ready.

Esther turned to the scene unfolding before them.

Madison stepped up to the reporter. Like the first time they had seen her, she was all dressed in black, except this time, her shoes and jewelry were gold. She had an expensive hat on, and her big hair was caught in a messy bun at the nape of her neck. Massive gold hoops were one of the three pairs of earrings she had on. Her lipstick was as gold as her jewelry.

"Madison Merriweather," Jack Jones began, "you're the best-selling author of *Blessed Be*."

Her collagen-filled lips pulled into a duck-lip smile. "Why yes," was all she offered.

"What brings a celebrity like you to the small town of Necanicum?" Jack asked.

She paused dramatically, waiting until she had everyone's complete attention. When it was silent she began.

"I am here to film *Blessed Be*, which will star Ransom and features my best friend Melissa Hearst-Stuart's beach home, and to release my latest novel, *Winter Solstice*." She broke into a Hollywood smile. Her daughter, Bridget, stood next to her, looking aloof.

"Can you tell us where Melissa Hearst-Stuart was and how you found her?" Jack Jones asked.

"Found her? Why, darling, she found me."

"Where were you last night and today? Why wasn't she here looking for her daughter?"

"That's enough," the chief said. Knowing he was on camera, he stepped between the reporter and the cameraman, eclipsing the live picture with his back. The cameraman shut down.

"Ms. Merriweather. I need you, your daughter, and the Stuart family to join me at . . . " He looked around at the numbers and hesitated for a minute. "At the Stuart beach castle," the chief said, unmistakably making a sarcastic remark about the size of the historic mansion the Stuarts lived in.

"And you," the chief said.

To Esther's surprise, he was talking to her. He turned, eyes not visible through his aviator glasses.

"You," he said again and pointed at Esther, Sophie, Nephi, and Bridget one at a time, "will join us for a little talk."

The Stuarts, Esther, Sophie, and Nephi became very sober. She felt like she had been summoned to the principal's office. But Madison wasn't intimidated.

"Officer, I have to meet my producer and director and see how far back this"—she waved a limp-wristed hand at the crowd and Cove—"will slow down our shoot today."

The chief, unaccustomed to being disobeyed, stood up taller, straightened his duty belt, put his hand on his cuffs, and said firmly, "You will come with me, one way or the other."

"Oh my." Madison touched her necklace. "Well, it looks like I will be coming for tea, Melissa," she said, completely ignoring the chief.

"Mommy, do we have to? This is boring," Bridget said.

"No baby, you run along and go shopping."

"Excuse me," the chief said. "You will also join this party."

"Humph," was all that came out of Madison.

The chief realized the cameraman was filming again.

"Thank you." The chief took away the camera. "You can pick this up at the station later today." He handed the equipment to a nearby officer, looked over his shoulder, and said, "Move it, people."

Startled, they all complied, walking together through the crowd and to the Stuart mansion.

# 17

# Read between the Lines

They left the crowd behind and passed the same green sedan. It hadn't moved, but the camera equipment was gone.

"I'm ready to go home and order a pizza," Nephi said.

"Are you ever not ready to order a pizza?" Sophie asked. "Guys? Isn't this the same green sedan? Do you suppose the driver lives around here?" She scanned the large, well-manicured houses, many of which were second homes or vacation homes, looking for anything that might indicate to whom the car belonged.

Esther didn't like to judge, but the little car didn't fit. "Maybe they broke down here when they were visiting the cove," she offered.

"What if they live in their car and want a nice neighborhood?" Nephi said.

"Whoa! You sounded as snobby as Bridget." Sophie gave him a playful push.

Bridget must have heard. She glanced back over her shoulder at them. Esther looked at the ground and felt her face grow hot.

When she finally looked up, the first thing she saw was Parker's mother walking arm in arm with Parker's dad. She leaned in and kissed her husband on the cheek and took Parker's hand. His dad looked at Parker with so much love in his face.

Parker bit his lip and looked worried.

"We will find her." He continued watching Parker's face while they walked. "I love you, son."

"I love you too. Both of you," Parker said easily.

Esther was close enough to hear them. She knew she should hang back and give them space, but she was fascinated.

*Is that what it's like?* Esther ached for love like that from a father. The ache was so raw and real; it was painful. *What is it like having a dad who loves you like that?*

Then Parker turned around, letting his parents and Bridget go on, and waited for her.

The closer she got to him, the more at peace her soul felt. She took the hand he offered her, and they walked toward his home.

# 18

# Never Judge a Book by Its Cover

Parker's father unlocked the door and let everyone in. The chief brought up the rear. They gathered under a vintage chandelier by the grand staircase.

"Shall we retire to the study?" Mr. Stuart said.

"All we need now is a butler named Jeeves," Sophie whispered.

"I need to freshen up," Melissa said to her husband.

She started going up the stairs, when the chief said, "Excuse me, ma'am."

"I'll be right back, I promise." She turned her back on him and continued on.

The chief took his hat off and scratched his head.

Mr. Stuart opened the door to the study, and they followed him in. He crossed the room and lit the fire with a push button. The house was warm, but Esther was still cold. She wasn't dressed for the cool weather.

"Mommy," Bridget whined. She leaned on her tall mother like a little girl.

Parker asked, "Do you want something to drink? Water? It's been a long day."

For some reason, his question made Esther's stomach growl. Parker walked over to the bookshelf and pulled a book back. The entire section of the bookshelves quietly swung open. Esther could see the kitchen and sitting room beyond.

Sophie slapped her forehead and said loud enough for everyone to hear, "Which way to the dungeon?"

Mr. Stuart let out a short laugh. "Good idea, Parker. Chief, would you like anything? Do you mind?"

The chief's expression was still hidden by the mirror glass in his sunglasses. He gave one nod and then stood by the fireplace.

Parker came back with an arm full of water bottles and a tin of butter cookies. Nephi took a bottle, and like a ravenous wolf snatched the tin, opening it and shoving two cookies in his mouth.

Parker set everything on a coffee table in front of the fireplace and then brought Esther water.

"I should be taking care of you," she said.

"I'm not hungry. All I can think about is, if Paisley isn't with Mum, then where is she?"

Esther realized that she hadn't puzzled out the ramifications of Mrs. Stuart's return without Paisley. They had hoped Paisley and her mother were together. If Paisley was alone, then she was in more danger. They needed to focus more on the beach, social media, and maybe even look at Bridget and Ransom, the actor. Paisley took so many selfies at the book launch, the party, and during her regular day.

Esther whispered to Sophie, "What if she captured something or someone in one of her pictures? Maybe her photos have a clue. You took some at the book launch we should look at too."

Her mind was reeling. There were so many possible motives for Paisley's disappearance. Maybe she had an accident. Maybe someone intentionally hurt her. Madison said she was upset that Paisley was missing but that this was interfering with her plans. But what if this was a publicity stunt? If it was, it was awful.

Sophie asked Parker, "Does your sister have a laptop or tablet?"

"She has a laptop."

"Can I see it?" Sophie said.

"It's in her room. Let me go get it." When he left the room, the chief actually rubbed his face with his hand in exasperation.

"Could everyone just take a seat?" he asked.

By the time everyone settled, Parker was back. He handed Sophie Paisley's laptop and cell phone.

Sophie looked like he had just handed her a million dollars. Greedily she took it over to the metal spiral staircase and sat down on the last step.

"Esther," she said. Esther looked longingly at Parker but joined her on the stairs. Not only could she see the laptop, but she had a bird's eye view of the chief.

"You're friends with Paisley on Facebook, right?" Sophie asked.

"Yes."

"Search her posts and comments. Look for anything unusual or a person that sounds angry. She's been gone almost a full twenty-four hours. If we don't find her today, the odds are bad for finding her," Sophie whispered to her.

"How do you know that?"

"I heard it on the *Real Crime* series on Netflix."

Esther rolled her eyes at Sophie and took out her phone to search.

"Good," Sophie said. "I knew it. Blondie uses the same password on all her accounts." She was already into the laptop and opening Instagram.

By the time Parker's mother returned to the room, Sophie and Esther were ticking through posts with thousands of likes, comments, and gifs. Each one had to be carefully reviewed. They hadn't even touched her YouTube account.

"Chief," Madison said, looking down her nose at the chief. "May we go first? I must get to my meeting."

"Okay," the chief said slowly. He looked at her for a full thirty seconds before he spoke again. "I am recording our conversation." He took the small recorder out of a leather container on his duty belt and laid it, running, on the table.

Madison drew her chin in and raised her eyebrows. Her plumped lips compressed into a straight line. Esther stopped searching social media. She couldn't look away. But Sophie, head down, kept digging. Out of the corner of her eye, Esther noticed Sophie was taking screenshots.

The chief did the same thing Detective Kohornen had. He stated the date, time, location, and the names of everyone in the room. It was pretty impressive. He had a great memory.

Then he looked directly at Madison. "When did you find out Paisley was missing?"

"What are you insinuating?" she said and put her hand over her heart. "I adore that girl."

"This will go faster if you answer my questions," the chief said.

"Well, I found out when Melissa did, as soon as we were back in cell service. A million messages loaded on my phone and hers. Then we saw the news alerts and the Amber Alert. Poor Melissa was absolutely frantic! My new cottage is a good twenty or so minutes down the coast, so we drove as fast as we could."

"You don't have any WIFI, cell service, or a landline at your new house?" the chief asked.

"No."

"And Bridget didn't deem it important enough to share with you when she returned home this morning? Can you please give me the address?" the chief asked. He wrote it down as Madison repeated it and then continued to question her.

"And it didn't occur to you to call someone? To pull over and let us know Melissa was with you?"

"We tried once, but the service is so spotty on the coast! You know how it is."

Bridget interrupted, "I don't want to stay there until we have WIFI. It's absolutely primitive."

"I wouldn't mind seeing her stay there another night," Esther said. She smiled at Sophie and winked.

She realized the chief was looking at her and looked down at the phone in her hand and kept scrolling.

The chief turned his attention back to Bridget and Madison. "Bridget, you told us that you thought something happened to Paisley and you suspected something had happened to Mrs. Stuart. Did you know she was at your mother's beach house?"

"Look," Sophie whispered. "She's trying to think." The chief frowned at Sophie.

"Shush," Esther said.

"I had no idea until I woke up this afternoon," Bridget said. "I was absolutely exhausted after last night, and I have a date later tonight with Ransom. After all, my life is what I need to focus on.

"When I left Paisley's, I drove back to my cottage and went straight back to bed. I was exhausted! Between your questions and texting Ransom to help him get through this . . . And then, Mother woke me early, like noon! Seriously.

"She said we had to take Melissa Stuart home and find someplace to eat lunch." Bridget stuck her bottom lip out, folded her arms, and looked away from the chief, indicating she was done talking. Apparently, the chief was also done talking to her.

Esther felt a fire start deep in her belly. The lies reminded her of long ago and gave her courage. Esther asked, "Where did you go after the fight?"

The chief's head snapped in Esther's direction. There was a moment of silence, while he shifted his weight, cocked his head in Bridget's direction, and folded his arms.

"Well?" The chief took a step toward Bridget. "Did you tell my officer you were out after you saw the Stuarts fight?" Silence.

Bridget pulled back deeper into the sofa and looked at the chief out of the corner of her eye.

"Answer the question."

Her nose rose in the air; she sat forward and stuck her chin out, puffy lips compressed. "You wouldn't understand."

"Try me."

"Ransom needed to know the truth. I couldn't have him involved in such a messy family. It could tarnish his reputation. I went to the cove to help him." She tilted her head and watched the chief, who let her stew for a moment. She folded her arms like the chief's and crossed her legs, squirming.

"So you met Ransom at the cove and he was with you?"

She looked down and deflated, looking at her mother for support, and said, "No. But I texted him."

She could have texted him from anywhere. She could have done something to Paisley to keep Ransom for herself. Esther gave Sophie a knowing look and raised her eyebrows.

Esther waited for the chief to ask Bridget more and find out what she did to Paisley.

"Miss Merriweather," the chief said, turning back to Madison. "You've been friends with the Stuarts for years. What kind of relationship does Paisley have with her parents?"

*Wait! Why isn't he asking Bridget more?* Esther looked at Sophie, her eyebrows gathered in concern, and shook her head from side to side. Sophie shrugged.

"Why, Paisley is the perfect child. They adore her. She can do no wrong," Madison said and joined Bridget in turning to look at anything other than the chief.

"If you are lying or interfering with this investigation in any way," the chief said, "then trust me, I will charge you with interfering with a law enforcement investigation."

Bridget looked back at the chief, still pouting. "There was this little person that kept bothering her online."

"Can you give me a description of the person, or are you just changing the subject?" the chief asked.

At that moment, Parker's mom opened the study door and came in looking like she'd just left a spa. She was in clean jeans and a white sweater. Her makeup, nails, and jewelry were perfect.

Madison motioned for Bridget to make room on the sofa with them, but Parker's mom said, "It's okay. I'll sit with Rob." She sat on the other couch by Parker's father.

Esther watched, fascinated that after everything, he put his arm around her and pulled her closer to him. There was no sign of the animosity she had seen last night.

"Mrs. Stuart," the chief started, "why didn't you call home last night or this morning? Did you know your daughter was missing?"

Melissa's serene face darkened. She drew in her chin and looked at her husband, as if she was searching for support. While she answered the chief, she never took her eyes off her husband's face.

Melissa said, "Paisley and I had brand new cell phones delivered." She pulled a mint green cell phone out of her jeans pocket and held it out to her husband. "I hadn't moved the data over. I know it is embarrassing, but I don't know your cell number. Madison had it, luckily.

All I took with me was my new phone with a credit card holder. So I took the credit card with me. I didn't think about cell service. I am so sorry, honey."

"I'm just glad you're okay." Mr. Stuart patted her hand and then held it.

"Mr. Stuart," the chief asked, "is it possible I have got a whole search and rescue crew out there working for nothing? Besides Bridget, does your daughter have other friends she might be staying with?"

"She might. I didn't know they had new cell phones. I saw the old one and assumed she left everything behind."

The chief's aviators hid most of his emotions. The chief began to pace. Any part of his face not covered by a mustache or aviator sunglasses gradually turned red.

"And you! Bridget," the chief said, visibly annoyed by everyone in the room. "Can you tell me more about the person who was bothering Paisley online?"

"He was at Mother's book signing. Did you see him, Mommy?" she asked. She stuck her lower lip out. Madison shook her head.

Bridget continued, "He's a professional photographer and wants to take her picture for a magazine. He even offered to get her an agent, but Paisley didn't like his style. I'm telling you, he was icky!"

The memory of the bald man with the pink lips in the bookstore went through Esther like lightning. And seeing the bald head in the sedan parked by their vehicle last night. A shiver ran up Esther's spine and she stood up.

"Sit down," the chief said.

Esther obeyed but leaned over to Sophie's ear and hissed, "Soph! I think I know who it is. We saw him!"

Sophie's eyes got wide behind her glasses. She turned the laptop so Esther could see the screen. She saw the man's face, with pink lips, staring back at her from an Instagram account. She pulled out her cell phone and scrolled through her photos. She turned the phone so Esther could see a selfie of Sophie at the book launch with the same man in the background. Bridget was nearby looking at him. She swiped the photo, and another took its place. It looked like Bridget was talking to him, or maybe shouting at him. He didn't show in the next picture. Sophie texted the pics to Esther so they both had them.

The chief walked closer to Bridget and bellowed, "Did he say a name? Can you tell me anything more about him?"

Bridget wrung her hands and tried to collect herself. She stuck her chin out and shook her head. "No."

# 19

# Children Are to Be Seen and Not Heard

While the chief sat quietly writing down all the details he had collected, Esther whispered in Sophie's ear, "We have to tell the chief. The green sedan must belong to the man in your selfie and Paisley's pictures."

"How do you know?" Sophie asked.

"I saw him drive it. I saw a bald head in it, the pink lips. I saw him at the bookstore. The pink lips both times." She wanted to scream at the chief—to make everything stop. Her stomach dropped the more the enormity of it sank deep inside her gut.

"Look," Sophie said. "She deleted some things, but I found these. Is this him?" She pointed at a string of private messages from someone whose username was @makeufamous. The city name under the username was Necanicum, their town. He was a local.

@Makeufamous asked, "Don't you want me to take you to go to New York and model to be famous? I promise this is for real."

Paisley Stuart replied, "Right! You're a total creeper. I am saving this thread. Not only should the grammar police arrest you, so should the crazy kiddy chaser cops. Stay away from me."

@Makufamous replied, "The police are my friends. Didn't you see my photo? I work for with the police. I am a mentor for youth."

Paisley Stuart replied, "This is your official warning. I called the crisis-line and told them all about you. I am going to get a stalking order and charge you with a crime if you contact me again—EVER!"

@Makufamous, "Listen," then he swore at her, "you played me. You want me only and I love you. Look at my feed. You knew I was watching. Now you'll ruin me, so I am going to ruin you."

Esther used her phone to photograph the messages on the laptop screen and save them.

"Besides the bad grammar and spelling, check this." Sophie switched to @Makufamous's page. The last picture was a photo of Paisley in her robe taken through a window at night. It was obviously taken in the Stuarts' Cape house. The window had green shutters and cedar shingles around it. It should have been a beautiful photo, but to Esther it was terrifying.

"Chief!" she said as she stood up. Then she realized the conversation in the room had gone on without her and she had interrupted.

"What!" he snapped.

Esther froze. Parker stood up and came to her side. He was frowning at the chief.

"You gotta see this." Sophie stepped in front of Esther. She handed the laptop to the chief who closed it.

"Sit down," he said. "You'll get your turn."

"You've got to look!" Sophie said. The chief tipped his head and scowled.

"You are interrupting my investigation."

"I am trying to help you, Chief. But if you don't want our help—come on Esther, let's go." Sophie marched for the kitchen door.

"Great. Leave. I'm not sure a crime even occurred," the chief called after her.

Not knowing what to do, Esther followed. Nephi stood up from his chair and joined them in the kitchen. They left Parker standing by the stairs with his mouth open.

# 20

# If All of Your Friends Jumped off a Bridge, Would You?

When they were far from the group, Sophie started digging through the kitchen drawers.

Nephi got close to her and whispered, "Sophie, what are you two doing? Did you find something?"

"Yeah, we did. Do you have it on your phone?" she asked Esther. Esther nodded. "We'll show you in a minute." Then Sophie pulled rubber gloves out of a drawer and plastic bags out of another. "Success," she announced. "Come on."

Sophie motioned for them to follow her out of the back door.

"We can't just leave Parker behind," Esther said.

"Esther loves Parker, Esther loves Parker." Nephi winked at her.

"I do not!"

"Listen, kids," Sophie said. "I won't buy you ice cream if you don't behave. Get with it, okay?"

Esther showed Nephi the photos of the social media messages, @makeufamous's photo of Paisley, and Sophie's selfies.

"Holy cow." Nephi's eyes grew big. When he finished reading them, she showed him the photo of Paisley in her room. All the color drained out of his face. And then just as fast, he was enraged. Nephi raised his fist and said, "I'm going to teach this guy how to fish as the bait. I'm going to hit him so hard he'll call me from tomorrow to apologize. I'm . . . "

"Good," Sophie said, "but first, we have to find him, and I know how."

"We're going to break into his car?" Esther asked. Her mouth fell open and her heart started to race.

"Listen, Esther, for Paisley's sake you gotta let go of being perfect. She needs us," Sophie begged. "And, Nephi, stay put. I want you to go back in there in about three minutes and get the chief to come and look at the car. Just give us time to get the registration and find an address for this guy."

"You're a genius," Esther said.

"Yes, I am. Now don't mess it up, Water Boy." Sophie smiled at Nephi as she slipped on yellow rubber kitchen gloves that were several sizes too large for her hands. "Come on," she motioned to Esther.

They sprinted to the green sedan. It had a red tow notice stuck on its windshield, dated today, from a local officer. Sophie ripped the notice off and stuck it in her pocket.

"Sophie!"

"If we don't take the sticker off, the guy that runs his tow truck around town will tow the car. What if the chief doesn't listen? I don't want to lose the car. Esther, why are you so afraid? Look, it isn't even locked. If you were missing, wouldn't you want someone to investigate your possible kidnapper? Better to ask—"

"I know—ask forgiveness than permission. It's just, the last thing I need is God to toss a lightning bolt at me." Esther joked to Sophie's back. She already had the passenger door open and was rifling through the glove box. She pulled out the registration and some mail, and took photos of it with the camera on her phone. "Man, this is awkward in these gloves. You take the pictures."

"No!" Esther stepped back. But then she saw the name and an address on the envelope. "Herbert Anderson? He lives right around the corner from me." The thought made her stomach roll. She took out her phone and took photos.

"Here they come." Sophie worked faster. The chief, Parker, and Nephi walked toward them, followed by the Stuarts.

"Quick, get your camera ready," Sophie said. She picked up the expensive-looking camera on the passenger seat and expertly turned it on. She showed Esther the digital feed on the back of the camera. It was full of photos Herbert had taken of Paisley. At the bookstore, on Christmas, in her bedroom window, running, and on the beach with the dog.

The tiny hairs on the back of Esther's neck rose as a chill ran down her spine. She said, "Herbert must have been doing this ever since they arrived in town."

"I'll take that." The chief reached for the camera.

Sophie pulled the camera back out of his reach. "Gloves, Chief!"

"Oh. Right. Thanks, Sophie. We should have a search warrant for this vehicle. But since it is an investigation and you already have everything in your hands, let's see what you've stolen."

"Are you going to arrest me?"

"No, but I might hire you."

Esther couldn't believe it. Sophie did everything she wanted to, said everything she couldn't, and always came out of it smelling like a rose.

"Take a look at this, Chief." Esther handed him Paisley's phone. "Sophie took these selfies, and look who is in the background. It's him, isn't it? What's Paisley's password again?"

"Sophie?" The chief shook his head. "Well, I guess the Stuarts—Parker anyway—knows you have the phone."

She navigated to the social media messages.

For the first time in Esther's memories, the chief removed the aviators and held the phone up to his face. He had blue eyes that were puffy and watering. *He must be as old as Grandma.*

His eyes grew larger, and his face grew redder as he mouthed the words to the texts.

"Wait, there's more." Sophie took the phone back.

"More?" he said incredulously. He took it back and looked at the photo of the bedroom window.

Parker and his parents looked over the chief's shoulder. His mother gasped and covered her mouth with her hand. All the color drained from her face while Mr. Stuart looked enraged. His face was bright red. Parker punched the side of the sedan, leaving a sizable dent in the passenger door.

"I'll pretend I didn't see that," the chief said, "because I want to shoot someone."

"We're wasting valuable time." Mr. Stuart gathered his wife in his arms. "What's next, Chief?"

"Sophie, did you see his address on the registration in the glovebox?" the chief asked.

"Yes." Sophie reached in and pulled the registration out and put it in a plastic bag for him.

The chief shook his head. "Sanoko Ito, Esther, Nephi, Parker, wait right here. I need to re-evaluate the search and telephone a judge for a search warrant of this man's house. Then I might offer you kids a job."

Sophie gave Esther a high-five.

The chief walked back to his squad car, talking to the Stuarts on the way.

"I'd better go with my parents," Parker said.

Sophie asked, "Do you want to go home?"

Parker nodded. "Yes. Even though I want to find this guy and give him a piece of my mind."

Sophie said, "I have a different idea, but I doubt the chief would be very happy about it. But don't tell the chief, Parker. I think we should check Herbert Anderson's house to see if Paisley is there."

Esther remembered how she felt when everything in her life was falling apart. She never knew what was going on, and her mom was always gone somewhere with Hart. She looked at Parker's exhausted face.

"Parker," Esther said. "I'm glad you're staying with your parents. Your mom just got home, and I'm sure she will want you with her. We can call you if we find anything. It won't take us long and we'll come back."

"I can't stop thinking about where Paisley is, but I know you're right," he said. "Every part of me wants to get this guy. Promise you'll call me if you find anything? And, Esther, please be careful."

"Pinky swear." Esther held up her pinky. He gave her a sad smile and then hugged her. She wanted to stop all of his hurt, like she wished someone would do for her. *Where were you when I was alone?*

Sophie high-fived Parker and he told her, "Take care of Nephi, okay?"

"Hey," Nephi protested.

But Parker just smiled. They left him at the corner and watched him walk back to his house.

✦ ✦ ✦

Esther, Sophie, and Nephi took the SUV to a small house a few blocks away from Esther's house.

Even though the street was in town, it was gravel with old-fashioned beach shacks in various stages of repair. At the end of the road was an unmarked gravel driveway that turned toward a nearby river, which fed into the ocean. They turned around and parked a block away.

"This has to be it," Esther said. "It isn't marked, but looking at the other addresses, it's the place."

Esther's phone vibrated. "It's Mom." She looked at Sophie with big eyes. "She's going to wonder where we are."

"Tell her you're hanging out with me. I told my parents I was sleeping over at your house again."

"Man, Esther, now who's going to be in trouble?" Nephi smiled. "I should text Hope after we check the house and let her know what's happening."

Sophie pulled the yellow kitchen gloves back on. "Remember, don't touch anything you don't have to. We're looking for Paisley, or any sign of her."

The gravel drive ran through tall laurel hedges mixed with pine trees. If there was a house, it wasn't visible from the street. It was getting late. Even though it was spring, the sun was already low in the sky, making the shadows long and the narrow road dark and cold.

They silently walked, side by side, on the gravel. Just as they lost sight of the street, the shrubs opened to a brown lawn. An old gray house sat in the middle of the yard. The paint was gone from most of the trim. The windows were dark, and moss grew on the roof. The front door was the only part of the house that led Esther to feel they were in the right place. It was painted hot pink.

"This guy has a thing for pink," Esther said.

Then they heard it. Sophie practically climbed up Nephi. It was a dog. A big dog. A low growl and a bark that was so deep Esther felt it go through her all the way to her toes. She ran.

Esther heard something behind her but was afraid to look back. She ran all the way to the main road before she realized it was Sophie and Nephi.

They gathered and caught their breath while the dog continued to bark. No one in the other houses seemed to notice. One house was dark, with a vacation rental sign on it. The other had the sounds of a loud television show leaking out of the windows.

Nothing had followed them.

Nephi started to walk. "I'm going back."

"Nephi," Sophie hissed, but he kept trudging, head down and determined.

"Whoa. He really likes her," Esther said.

The dog barked louder and louder, until it reached a frenzied pitch. They heard Nephi saying something, but it was hard to understand over the barking. Then it stopped.

Sophie and Esther looked at each other, mouths open, afraid to breathe.

"I guess we should go see what happened to him," Esther said.

They started to walk as quietly as they could until they reached the clearing. They both waited. Still, no barking.

Nephi came around from the back of the house, with a wide grin on his face. "It's all clear," he yelled.

"What happened?" Esther asked.

"Come see my new friend," Nephi motioned. They followed him to a dog kennel behind the house. A black and white Pitbull was eating a big pile of dog food poured through the fence. "No one came to see why he's barking, so I doubt anyone is in the house. I don't think anyone has fed him in a day or so. His water dish was empty too. I found food in that shed and used the hose. Poor little puppy."

"Poor little puppy?" Sophie said. "That thing is a horse."

"Come on," Esther said. "I feel like the chief will be here any minute. What are we looking for? What if he's inside and just didn't come out?"

"He can't be." Nephi shook his head. "He would've come out when the dog barked. What should we call the dog?"

"Nephi! He could still be in there with Paisley. We're trespassing. Did you knock?" Esther asked.

"No. Let's go see if he's here. I want to have a little talk with him." Nephi strode off toward the front of the house.

He knocked and the girls stood at the bottom of three cement stairs, ready to run.

They waited.

Nothing.

"See, no one's home," Nephi said. He reached out and turned the handle with his bare hands. "Locked." Sophie held the yellow gloves out for him.

Then they heard the sound of tires on the gravel. They ran toward the river and stood behind the large laurel and watched. A police cruiser, lights on, entered the clearing. The dog started barking again. The driver's window rolled down.

The officer radioed, "Six thirteen out at the suspect's residence. Code four at this time. Waiting for my second."

The tall officer got out of the vehicle and walked behind the house but went right back to his car. A second police unit drove up the driveway. Gustafson, the young officer from the beach, joined the tall officer.

They watched as the tall officer made a call on his mobile phone.

"Hi, Chief. There's a big dog here, barking in a kennel, so if he's here, he knows we are . . . No signs of life . . . We will."

The officers unsnapped their weapons and approached the doorway off to the side. The tall officer was in front and Gustafson crouched behind him. The lead officer reached out, without standing in front of the door and knocked.

"Anderson! Herbert Anderson!" he called.

Nothing. The dog continued to bark. Eventually they backed up and looked in the large front window.

They retreated to their vehicles. The tall one stood with his vehicle between him and the house. He made a call.

"Chief? No answer. I really don't think he's here. I know." He hung up and walked to Gustafson's vehicle. He leaned on the window. "Chief says to be vigilant. We're parked until we get a search warrant. Do you want to go back out and wait at the entrance to the drive?" He nodded and saluted Gustafson as he backed up the driveway.

"Why don't they just go in?" Nephi whispered.

"Better question," Esther said, "how are we going to get out of here and get back to the car without getting shot? It's dark."

"We can go along the river," Nephi said.

"Are you sure?" Sophie asked.

"It's how I used to sneak out to go to bonfires." His white teeth flashed in the dark. "Come on."

# 21

# Beg, Borrow, or Steal

It was an hour before they returned to Parker's house. They stopped at Esther's house to change into fresh clothes. Covered in river mud, they slipped in the back door and left their muddy things on the porch to avoid getting caught.

Sophie put on Esther's little sister's shoes and they fit. So did her Mickey Mouse hoodie and black leggings.

They left Hart's keys on the counter and took Mable's old truck back.

When they passed the cove, they realized all the search and rescue vehicles were gone. The beach was completely empty. Only one car with a young couple sat in the parking lot.

"They've stopped looking for her," Nephi said in frustration. "How can they?"

"They're still searching," Esther answered. "Just not here."

They rounded the corner and saw a police cruiser parked a block away from the sedan.

Esther pointed it out. "They must be waiting for a warrant too."

"Should we knock on the door?" Sophie asked. The lights were on in the Stuart house, but the chief's car was gone.

"Let me text Parker," Nephi said.

They didn't have to wait long before Parker answered. He joined them on the porch, quietly closing the door behind him.

He gave Nephi a buddy hug and hugged Sophie. He put his arm on Esther's shoulder and gathered her in, like his father had pulled his mother closer to him. *Like this is normal,* Esther thought. It was the first time she had let a boy this close, but she wasn't about to tell Parker.

"Did you find anything?" he asked.

"Nothing. Sorry, buddy. How are your parents?" Nephi asked.

"They're really scared. My mom keeps crying. Madison stayed at the house for a while to comfort her but then said she couldn't miss her meeting. I was so glad to see Bridget leave."

"Do you know what's happening?" Sophie asked.

"They tried the Find Your Phone app to locate Paisley's phone, but they only found the one she left behind. If she has the other one, it must be dead. They're waiting for a search warrant for the car and the guy's house. They put something out so that if an officer sees him, they'll pick him up." Parker frowned.

"He isn't at his house," Esther said.

"How did it go?"

"We couldn't get inside." Nephi looked at the ground.

"You didn't miss a thing, except the dog from the devil's house and a creepy old shack. It's empty. At least I hope it is," Sophie said.

# 22

# You're Nobody until Somebody Loves You

"So what do we do now?" Parker asked. "I can't stand all this waiting."

Sophie said, "Let me look up her social media accounts on my phone and see . . . "

Sophie was cut off when the chief's car rounded the corner and headed their way. It passed them going fast and continued toward the cove. Without talking they all ran down the porch steps and jumped in the old truck. Parker rode in the back. Nephi pulled out and tried to catch up with the chief.

He didn't have to go far. The chief's car was parked in the cove parking lot with the lights on. The chief was already down the rocks with a flashlight. The streetlights and moon cast just enough light for them to see something in the surf. The chief knelt by it and was talking to a couple.

The man had his arm around the woman, who had her head buried in his shoulder.

"What is that?" Parker asked. He jumped out of the truck and walked over to them.

No one answered him. He stepped closer and saw the body rolling in the surf.

They heard sirens coming in the distance. The man helped the woman up the rocks.

"Who is it?" Parker asked.

"A body!" the woman cried out. The man pulled her to himself.

"It's awful," he said. "It's been in the water a long time. Don't go down there."

Parker collapsed to his knees. Esther fell beside him and put her arms around him, buried her head in his neck. "We don't know. Don't lose hope. Hang on!"

Another police car and an ambulance, lights on, parked. Officers jogged down to meet the chief and help pull the body up onto the sand.

A woman in a car pulled up and got out.

"Don't go down there," Sophie told her.

"It's okay," she said. She gave Sophie a sad smile. "I'm the medical examiner."

Esther, Sophie, Parker, and Nephi waited for the chief to leave the beach and talk to them. Parker hadn't said a word. He stared blankly at the spotlights the officers were setting up on the beach. His arms were folded, and he was chewing on his bottom lip.

Nephi and Sophie sat on the tailgate of Nephi's old truck. Esther clung silently to Parker's hand. They leaned against the bed of the truck. Sophie was frantically digging through Paisley's social media looking for any new posts or sign that she was still alive.

Esther's phone chimed. A text. "Hey, you okay? Can I come help? This is Joe" *Joe? Oh, Joe Hart.* It was from Hart?

She didn't know what to say. She didn't respond. *You're not my dad.* She looked at Parker, who was pacing, and put her phone back in her pocket.

An older deputy introduced himself to them as Davis. He took their information and asked them to wait. County deputies set up crime scene tape and cones, closing off the parking lot. The lights on the chief's car silently flashed red and blue beside an idling ambulance.

Nephi stood up and began to pace without taking his eyes off the scene unfolding in front of them. His hands were balled into fists.

"There are officers from three towns and the county here. It must be more than a fisherman overboard."

Parker spoke for the first time, "What am I going to tell my parents? I need to go home." Esther put an arm around his shoulder, wishing she could do something to ease his fears. She couldn't say everything would be okay. She knew from experience sometimes it gets worse before it gets better.

Sophie growled in frustration and put her phone down on the tailgate. Getting up, she said, "We need information." She started toward the beach. Esther and Parker followed.

The county deputy stepped in their path.

"Can we see the chief?" Sophie asked. "We want to know who that is." She pointed at the body lying just out of the surf. The medical examiner knelt by it and the chief stood over it.

One corner of Deputy Davis's mouth lifted. He put his hands on his hips and looked down at Sophie, an angry little girl in a Mickey Mouse sweatshirt.

Davis said, "We would like to know too. When we can, we'll release the information."

Sophie tried to push past him. He caught her by the hood, picked her up under her arms, turned her around, and sent her back to Esther and the boys.

"Argh," she growled. "Nephi, use your brawn and get us some information!"

Parker shook his head, his mouth drawn down, his shoulders slumped. "I need to go talk to my parents." He started walking. Esther's eyes opened wide. She shook her head at Sophie and Nephi, and motioned for them to follow him.

"Wait," she called to Parker. "What are you going to tell them?"

He didn't turn around. He shrugged and kept going. They caught up and walked together.

"I don't think it's her," Sophie offered. "If it was Paisley, the chief would have talked to you. He'd be on his way to your parents."

Parker paused for a moment, tipped his head, and looked thoughtfully at Sophie. "I hope so. Still, I should let them know." He began walking toward home.

# 23
# The Long Road Home

When they arrived, Parker pushed open the gate. Esther followed and said, “Parker? Do you want us to come in with you?”

With his hand still on the gate, he looked over his shoulder. “I probably should go in alone.”

Without thinking she offered, “We’ll wait out here, okay? Just text us if you need us.” She stepped back and let the gate close.

“Let’s go sit on the porch. There are lots of chairs.” Sophie went through the gate.

A light went on inside the house. The front door was a large double door with oval windows on both sides. Stained glass windows with pictures of an angry ocean and ships were on either side of the doors. Curtains on the oval windows prevented them from seeing anything inside. Random groupings of chairs and potted plants decorated the porch.

Esther thought she heard something coming from inside the house, a sound of anguish. They all froze, looking at the door. After a few quiet moments, she found three oversized wicker chairs in a grouping. They sat down and waited.

# 24

# Left in the Dark

It wasn't long before the chief's vehicle pulled up in front of the house.

He came up the walk and saw them on the porch. Walking up the stairs to the door, he asked them before he knocked, "Are you waiting?"

"Yes," was all Esther offered.

He nodded. "You know it's getting late. Does your mom know you're here?"

Esther nodded. *Another lie!* Sophie poked her in the ribs with her elbow but didn't say anything.

The chief knocked. Parker opened the door and let the chief in. Parker looked at Esther. His face was so sad, as if the weight of the world rested on his shoulders. The door closed and they all looked at each other.

"What?" she said to Sophie and Nephi. "I'm not leaving him here. I wouldn't leave you." No one said a word.

It wasn't long before the chief came back out of the house. The Stuarts followed him onto the porch.

"I'm sorry if it caused you any concern. We will let you know as soon as we do. We should have a warrant shortly," the chief said, his hat in his hands.

Mr. Stuart said, "Thanks, Chief. We won't' sleep until she's home."

The chief stopped and looked at Mr. Stuart for a moment. "No, I don't believe you will."

"Good night," Melissa said, and shook the chief's hand. He put his hat on and walked down the porch to his cruiser and pulled away.

Mrs. Stuart turned to Esther and the kids and asked, "Won't your mothers be worried?"

Sophie stood up. "They know where we are. Parker is too important for us to leave him alone."

Parker's mother's eyes looked puzzled, but his father just smiled. "Then why don't you come in? We aren't very hungry, but I can order some pizzas for you."

Parker was waiting in the entryway. They went into the study and sat on the couches by the fire.

"Give me your phone," Sophie said to Esther. Esther handed Sophie her cell phone, and Sophie punched in Esther's pass code and texted someone.

"Who was that?" Esther asked.

"Your mom. You're sleeping over with me."

For once, Esther was grateful for Sophie's wild ways. Then her phone vibrated. It was a text from her mother, Grace. It read, "Hart says they found something at the cove. Might want to text Parker and make sure he's okay."

Her mom knew everything and everyone. She probably knew exactly where they were. *I am in so much trouble,* Esther thought.

Esther replied to her mom, "Might come home later. I'm with Sophie and Parker now." *At least,* she thought, *I'm almost honest.*

But her stomach nagged at her. It was as if someone was whispering in her ear, *Don't lie to your mother, even an almost lie.* It wouldn't let up, even when Parker put his arm around her and she snuggled in by the fire.

"What did the chief say?" Esther asked.

Parker offered, "He just said they don't know who it is, but he doesn't believe it is Paisley and he didn't want us to worry. He couldn't release the name even if he had it, until he notified the next of kin.

"He promised he would tell us if they turned up anything about Paisley. He thinks they'll have a warrant soon now that there is an unidentified body."

They sat in silence for a few more minutes.

Parker's father brought in the pizzas when they were delivered, along with some root beer. But no one touched it. Esther wasn't hungry, and she doubted Parker was either.

"We should go," Nephi said quietly. "I know this won't make sense, but I don't have a bad feeling. I think we're going to find her."

"All I feel is fear—dark black fear." Parker leaned forward, rubbing his eyes with both hands.

"Do you want us to stay?" Esther asked.

He took her hand. "Please?" was all he said.

Esther raised one eyebrow at Nephi and then motioned with her head for him to sit down.

"I'm starving." He pulled out a slice of pizza, rolled it, and ate it in three bites. While he was still chewing he poured himself a glass of root beer. Esther made another face at him, eyebrows raised, lips pressed in a mom face.

"What?" he said. "His dad wants us to eat."

The door to the study opened, and Parker's mother and father came in. They looked tired and older somehow but were smiling.

"It isn't Paisley," his father announced.

Parker fell back on the sofa and put his hands over his face. Esther heard a muffled sob. It actually sounded like he was crying.

His hands dropped and Parker leaned forward, wiping a tear from the corner of his eye. "I am so relieved."

"It's a man. That's the good news," his father continued, "if it can be good news. But, the bad news is, they think it is Herbert Anderson. And if he's dead, where is she?"

"We need to go back out and look for her and Cornwallis," Nephi said.

"Not tonight," Parker's mother said. "We don't know what's going on out there, but it's late and I can't have another missing person on my conscience."

"Do you care if we wait to see if they have any more news?" Nephi asked.

"Of course not," Mr. Stuart said. "We'll be in the kitchen or upstairs if you need us." She walked to Parker and they hugged. Mr. Stuart put a protective arm around her as they left the study.

They sat back down on the couches. Esther was grateful for the fire. After he filled up, Nephi stretched out on a couch and fell asleep.

Parker had only eaten a few bites. Esther managed a few bites and a trip to the bathroom. When she came back, she found Parker asleep on the other couch and Sophie asleep on a rug in front of the fireplace.

Esther laid on the third couch and watched the flames of the gas log. She wondered how they could all sleep. All she could do was review the events of the last twenty-four hours over and over again.

Finally, as the sun peeked over the mountains to the east and birds began to sing, Esther dozed off.

*She was running, trying to keep up with the long distance track team. They crossed the beach along the shoreline and then finally made it to rocks near the parking lot at the cove.*

*Paisley climbed nimbly and sprinted ahead. A dark green sedan rumbled to life. She ran to warn Paisley. Paisley was already up the hill.*

*She had to run faster. The sedan passed her. A bald head with bright pink lipstick smiled at her. Where his eyes should have been were dark holes.*

*She tried to run faster, but the road became soft like sand. With every step she took it shifted and she couldn't get any momentum. Paisley left the road and followed the gravel trail into the woods.*

*She had to stop her. She tried to call out, but she couldn't make a sound and her feet felt like lead, sinking in sand.*

*Then she saw him. Ahead of Paisley, behind a log, pink lips smiling, camera ready.*

*"Paisley, look out! Paisley!" she tried to call, but no sound came out of her mouth. She wanted to warn her, but she couldn't speak. Then she tried again. "Paisley, Paisley . . . "*

# 25

# East West Home's Best

Esther woke up with a start and sat up on the couch. She didn't have her glasses on, but she could see well enough to know thankfully she was the only one awake.

*What woke me up?* she thought.

There it was again. A dog was barking and scratching at the French doors. He whined and she ran to the doors

"Parker, Parker! Wake up!" she said. "It's Cornwallis! He's back!"

Parker stood up and wiped the sleep from his eyes. A smile spread across his face, and he opened the doors, letting Cornwallis knock him down and lick him.

Sophie and Nephi rubbed the sleep from their eyes and watched Parker and Cornwallis's reunion. There were branches, leaves, and dirt stuck all over the dog's matted hair. He had dried blood on one leg and was favoring it. He held the paw up and walked like a tripod on three legs.

Even with the injured leg, Cornwallis was wild with joy. He wagged his tail with his whole body and jumped on Parker, who didn't stop him. They rolled on the ground together.

"Where were you, boy? Where were you, boy?" Parker asked the dog.

Cornwallis barked and jumped.

"No!" Sophie said. "This isn't one of those dogs who is going to take us to Paisley, is it?"

"Of course, it is!" Esther dodged a dog kiss. "We need something that belongs to Paisley."

Cornwallis barked again.

"Are you hungry, boy? Let me feed him first." Parker rubbed the dog's back. Cornwallis followed him, leaping several feet off the ground and still barking. "Where have you been? You're a good boy." Parker opened a cupboard and pulled out a bag of dog food and put a scoop in Cornwallis's bowl. The dog immediately ate it like he hadn't eaten in days.

Sophie darted out of the kitchen and returned with a shirt. "This must be Paisley's shirt," she said to Esther. "It was in the laundry room hamper. It says Oceanside High, but it's pink."

Parker looked at them and asked, "Do you really think that will work? This isn't a movie."

"What have we got to lose?" Esther asked. "You told me Cornwallis was smart."

Nephi shrugged. "I agree. What have you got to lose?"

"Give me the shirt." Parker rubbed it on Cornwallis's nose. "Go get her, boy. Go get her!"

Cornwallis took off at a full run for the French doors in the study. He was outside before they even moved.

Mouths opened, they looked at each other and Sophie yelled, "Run!"

Cornwallis was out of sight by the time they hit the back yard, but they could hear him barking. They ran to the front of the house and saw his retreating form a full quarter of a mile ahead of them on the road to the cove.

"I'll get the truck!" Nephi yelled. He ran off the opposite way of the dog.

Sophie took off at a full run, racing to catch up. Parker wasn't far behind her.

Esther ran behind them, the adrenaline pumping in her system. Emotions ran through her, pumping with her heart. Fear she would lose Parker and Sophie, and anger at Herbert Anderson and anyone like him, fueled her run. Horror at what they might find when they caught up with the dog kept her from feeling her lungs burn. She had heard of dogs staying with their injured master long after they had died.

Nephi pulled alongside her in the truck. She climbed in and the truck roared to life as they tried to catch up with Sophie and Parker. They couldn't see Cornwallis.

"This is the way Paisley runs," Nephi shouted over the motor. It wasn't long before they reached the parking lot at the top of the hill.

Parker and Sophie left the pavement and took the gravel trail that ran six miles over the mountain to the next town. They disappeared from sight in the dense Oregon forest almost immediately.

# 26

# Dog Tired

Esther knew the trail well. She, Nephi, and their family took it annually, with her Grandma Mable in the lead. It twisted and wound through the woods until you emerged from the trees at the viewpoint. From the viewpoint it was a three-hundred-foot or more drop to the ocean and rocks below, and in the distance you could see a light house on an island. Beyond the light house the ocean was so vast it made Esther feel small.

One year they had spotted a black bear and had cancelled the hike. Since then, she always hiked with her eyes wide open. There were mountain lions and elk the size of horses on the mountain. Her sister's constant chatter and the size and noise their group usually made her feel safe. She couldn't imagine being on the mountain alone, injured . . . or worse.

Nephi didn't bother rolling up the windows or locking the truck. He ran to catch up with Parker. Esther was hot on his heels. Slipping on the gravel trail, she regretted wearing cute shoes that weren't designed for running.

The trail was still damp from the winter rains. Although it was spring, it was dark under the canopy of trees. There were whole sections of the trail that were completely muddy. Cornwallis's footprints showed clearly in the mud, and she could hear him barking in the distance.

The trail became a series of switchbacks, climbing higher and higher. Esther's lungs were burning but she didn't care. She caught up to Nephi, who was climbing over a fallen tree blocking the trail.

The tree was covered in moss, and even on its side it was as tall as she was. It must have fallen recently. The roots were still covered in dirt, like a plate pulled from the ground.

Nephi stopped on the other side and called to her, "You have to go the way the dog went."

She looked down and realized the dog had gone down onto the slippery hillside and under the tree. She took a firm hold on a handful of lush fern leaves. Plant by plant, she slid and climbed under the tree, emerging on the other side.

"That's a widowmaker," she said to Nephi as he helped her up the other side. He didn't answer but turned and kept trotting and running up the mountain ahead of her. Each of them breathed heavily and rhythmically.

The barking was sounding farther and farther away.

"Why would she come all this way in the dark?" Esther called out.

"No clue!" he yelled. A moment later, they reached another bend in the trail. "I would never have looked up here. How did the leash get in the ocean?"

A jolt ran through Esther, and unbelievably, a new burst of adrenaline ran through her body. She knew.

"The cliffs!" she said.

Nephi's eyes got wide and his mouth fell open. He took off running with renewed speed.

Esther followed, but something inside her was losing hope. She knew this mountain like the back of her hand.

# 27

# Stop Crying or I'll Give You Something to Cry About

During World War II, the mountain had been an Army lookout after a Japanese submarine bombed the Oregon coast. Soldiers lived in cement bunkers on the cliffs and mountaintop. One bunker was a series of tunnels that ran deep into the ground. Esther's family had explored the bunkers with flashlights when Esther was young. Now there was a metal gate over the entrance, and the exit had a manhole cover.

Paisley could be anywhere. But if the leash was in the water, maybe she was too.

The sun showed through the pines. But in the early morning hours and on this side of the hill there were a lot of shadows. Esther tripped over a root and slipped on rock, tearing the skin on her knee.

Shocked, she sat for a moment holding her knee. Nephi turned around and was coming back for her when she waved him on, "Go! Go! I'm all right."

She got up and tested the knee. It was bleeding down her shin, but the injury seemed to be superficial. She began running again and berating herself for not being a better athlete. *What is wrong with you?*

"God," she said out loud. "Make me a better runner for my friend, Paisley." *My friend? The one thing I should do for God was stop judging girls like Paisley.*

"Guys!" Esther could hear Sophie yelling from somewhere in the distance. Suddenly she forgot her burning lungs. She forgot to think about her legs or breathing or anything. She thought, *This must be a runner's high.*

She caught up with Nephi and was easily pacing him. They must have gone more than a mile and were coming up on two when the trail changed. It opened into a field of white daisies and winding dirt trails in all directions.

She knew this place and kept to the well-worn path. Then she heard Sophie again. "Guys! Over here!"

Cornwallis barked, and Parker came back down the trail toward them.

When he caught up to them, between breaths, Parker said, "We found a cement hole or kind of a cave. Sophie says it's a bunker. The dog won't go in, but the door had a padlock that is just lying on the ground. Come on. Bunker."

Taking a side trail, Parker took off running. Esther took her headband out of her hair and hung it on a tree. It was a spot of bright yellow to tell her where they turned off the main trail. Then she followed Parker and Nephi toward the cliffs.

They didn't run far before the trial turned again. It dipped and then climbed. It was covered in foliage. A blackberry bush scraped her bare arms and tore a hole in her shirt.

She heard Nephi ahead.

"Crepes!" He used Sophie's favorite word.

She caught up to him and looked at what Parker had described. They all stood at a six-foot-high and three-foot-wide door. Someone had put an iron door over the opening, probably to keep kids like them out of it. The door was open. A low moan came through the door, and then a gust of wind that smelled of urine made Esther close her eyes and gag.

# 28

# There's Nothing under Your Bed or in the Closet

Esther made eye contact with Parker. "Is she in there?"

"We haven't gone in. We called out and didn't get an answer. Cornwallis barked and without a doubt didn't want to have anything to do with the tunnel." Sophie was crouched beside the dog and trying to calm him.

The tunnel or room was pitch black inches inside the door.

"Does anyone have a flashlight or lighter?" Nephi asked.

Esther pulled her cell phone out of her back pocket and turned on the flashlight, shining it into the dark hole. It ate the light.

"Paisley!" Nephi bellowed. Nothing.

"If she's here, wouldn't she be calling for help?" Sophie asked, looking at them from the ground, where she was holding the dog.

*If she can,* Esther thought, but didn't say it out loud. She studied Parker's face for a moment. He held his hand out to her, and she put the phone in it.

Parker took a deep breath and crossed the threshold, entering the tunnel. Esther put both her hands on his shoulders. She hid her face behind his neck and tried to only breathe the musky scent of his sweat and ignore the other smells.

There was water on the floor that seeped into her shoes. Parker slipped and almost took them down. The tunnel sloped gently into the earth. Water ran in little rivulets through cracks in the walls. Finally the tunnel leveled for a few feet and then turned.

They couldn't see beyond the circle of their light. *It must be large, she thought.* Another gust of wind created a moan that sounded like a person as it blew somewhere in the distance. Wind blew through the room and through her loose hair, making her bury her nose in his hair to avoid the smell.

Parker hesitated for a moment and went to the left. He let the light follow the wall in the room. There was a cement indent about waist-high and the length of a bunk. Then they passed a well-used fireplace cut into the cement, another bunk. A small room, only big enough for a man and a desk, opened off the wall, but it was empty other than a brown blanket. It looked like something had slept in it. Esther guessed the main room was a good thirty or forty feet long.

Finally they reached another door. They left the room and walked up what looked like another long sloping hall. This time it climbed. At the end of it, they could see a round opening, like a manhole cover with light faintly seeping in around the edges. It looked empty, but Parker went halfway up to be sure. The wind blew around the cover and created the same moaning sound, sending shivers up Esther's spine.

She heard something skitter and whispered, "Is that a rat?" Her whispered voice echoed through the chamber. The skittering got louder and then stopped.

"Whatever it was, I hope you scared it away," Parker whispered back. Again it sounded like he was talking in an echo chamber. They followed the other wall back toward the opening of the bunker. It had three more small rooms and one more bunk. Then they saw it.

A neat and clean pink blanket was laid out on the bunk with a candle. The rat Esther heard was nesting on the blanket with little blind babies. A hydro-pack, or runners pack with water in it, was on the floor. As they scanned the area, the low battery warning flashed on the cell phone.

Parker grabbed the pack before they headed back toward the entrance.

Picking up the pace, they all but ran to the sunlight.

"Did you see anything?" Sophie asked.

"No, but I found this. I'm sure it's hers." Parker's entire body was shaking. Tremors in his hands shook the hydro-pack he held. His eyes bulged and he sounded like he was going to hyperventilate. Sweat traced a path in a spot of dirt on his cheek.

Esther took the pack from his hand as he bent over and looked like he was going to pass out. Her hands shook as she opened the pack and pulled out a brand new pink cell phone, without a scratch or sign of wear. It was in a clear glitter case with a twenty-dollar bill tucked between the case and the phone. She tried to turn it on, but the battery was dead.

"It has to be hers," Nephi stated the obvious. Esther could hear the anguish in his raspy voice. The wind blew through the tunnel, and somewhere in the distance she heard a twig snap. She jumped, every sense in her body on high alert.

"You don't think he's still here, do you?"

Parker's face turned from fear to rage, "No, he's dead." He stood up, and Esther recognized something familiar—the need to fight because you're so afraid that you're sure you're going to die.

"Let the dog go, Sophie," Parker ordered.

Sophie's eyes matched her round glasses. She closed her mouth and then stood up, releasing Cornwallis, who ran as if his life depended on it. Not back to the trail, but straight toward the cliffs.

"Cornwallis!" Esther screamed. "Cornwallis!" She began sprinting. She called over her shoulder, "The cliffs! He'll die!"

Only twenty feet ahead of her the dog came to a halt and began pacing back and forth. Esther saw something familiar to Oregonians who lived on the coast.

On the coast, a highway, a cliff, or even someone's backyard could be stable for years. Meanwhile, little underground streams formed by the constant rains and run-off cut away at rock like a knife through pie.

The side of the cliff looked like someone had taken a giant pie cutter and sliced a piece off. The ragged earth and torn shrubs were in a perfect V-shape. Rocks and raw soil below the grass and plants meant to protect the cliff had washed away from soil erosion. The groundwater had won. A piece of the mountain had sloughed off and fallen two to three hundred feet to the rocks and the ocean below.

"Cornwallis," Parker called. He joined Esther. Cornwallis paced back and forth along the raw dirt.

Esther put her arm across Parker's chest. "Don't move a step more. There's a good chance this ground is soft and there is nothing below it. You could fall to your death." She got down on her knees and realized Sophie had joined her.

"Stay back, Sophie," she said quietly. Everyone stood behind her. She started to call the dog.

"Cornwallis, here, boy." She whistled. They all called the dog, who kept pacing back and forth and looking at them but wouldn't come. He wouldn't even respond to Parker. Finally he laid down along the ragged edge of raw dirt. He panted and whined, looking at them and then out to sea.

Esther knew what she had to do. Laying on her stomach, she inched across the ground to the edge of the cliff. Somehow spreading her body weight out, like she was crossing thin ice, felt right.

Feeling the rocks and plants tear her leg up didn't stop her. She continued to slowly slide forward, pulling herself with her hands and pushing with her toes. She waited for the ground to give way under her. When Cornwallis was panting above her head, she was at the edge of the cliff. The ocean spread out to the horizon ahead of her.

For a moment, she caught her breath and listened. In the distance, below her, she could hear the tide crashing on the rocks, over and over again. Then she heard something else, a sound that didn't belong, but was muffled by Sophie's cries for her to stop.

She pushed herself a little further forward. Sophie was yelling for her to come back, but she ignored her. Gradually she peeked over the edge. A rock the size of her fist dislodged and fell, hitting other rocks, and then . . .

"Ow!"

Esther pushed herself further forward and looked over the edge. Paisley looked up at her from a small ledge. She was huddled up against the mountain side, squatting, holding her ankle.

"Paisley!" she called. Gravel and rocks dislodged and rained down on Paisley's blonde hair. Paisley smiled through cracked lips. Her face was badly sunburned, and her eyes were swollen almost shut. She started to say something and almost lost her balance.

"Don't move! Don't talk! I'll be back!" Esther pushed back and called in triumph, "We found her! She's alive!"

Parker fell to his knees and openly wept. Nephi slapped him on the back in joy, and Sophie punched her fist in the air.

# 29

# It's My Way or the Highway

Nephi was the first to speak again. "How are we going to get her up from there?"

Parker started toward the edge.

"Stop!" Esther called. "Every step in that direction sends rocks down on her head. You have to stay back."

He stepped back and then took several deep breaths, trying to pull himself together. "We have to get her off the cliff. She needs to know I'm here."

"The best thing you can do is let her concentrate on not falling." Esther held Sophie's phone up, trying to get service. "No bars and less than ten percent battery. Sophie, run back down the mountain until you see bars. I couldn't get any cell service up here with your phone. As soon as you have service, call nine-one-one. We need the high angle rescue team or the coast guard. I don't know how long she can hold on."

Her last statement sent another wave of anguish across Parker's face. He looked at Esther and asked, "What if Sophie gets lost? How can she lead them back here?"

"Nephi," Esther ordered. "Go with Sophie. I marked a tree on the trail with my yellow headband. Don't get lost!"

Nephi and Sophie took off running for all they were worth, Sophie was ten steps ahead until they were out of sight.

It became quiet. The only sounds were Cornwallis's panting and the ocean tide. Esther sat down on a mossy log, and Parker sat silently next to her.

"How does she look? Is she okay?" he asked

"I think her ankle might be broken. She's sunburned but she smiled at me. She's far enough down, she could barely hear me." Esther smiled, and reached out and took his hand. "But I think she's going to be fine once they reach her."

"How can they, if the cliff side is still giving way? I feel so helpless." He stood and paced for a minute.

Esther closed her eyes and thought, *Dear God, help us. Help Paisley. Please.* She remembered looking at Paisley at the book signing and being . . . what? Jealous? All those feelings melted away. *Forgive me for thinking ill of her. Forgive me. Let her live for Parker. I'll be better.*

"Parker?" Esther asked. "Tell me about Paisley."

He smiled and looked at the ocean. "We have this funny connection. I've always been the big brother even though I am only minutes older, so I rub it in, but I also feel protective of her. She acts tough, but she's not." He looked back at Esther and then sat down by her.

"I remember this one time, we were little, and we wandered off. We were supposed to be in the stables while Mom saddled our ponies. But she saw a cat and followed it. I still remember chasing her chasing the cat.

"And then, we were lost in the woods. Massive trees and the two of us holding hands and crying. We were probably only twenty feet from the house, but it felt like miles." Parker paused and looked at his feet. "Just like this."

"What did you do?"

"I was the hero. I found the way home. She still wants me whenever she feels lost. And I look to her to make me laugh. You should see her impression of Madison Merriweather." A sad half-smile settled on his face.

Cornwallis left his post and put his head in Parker's lap.

# 30

# The Waiting Game

The more time passed, the more anxious Esther got. She paced. Her thoughts raced. *What if something happened to Sophie? What if it took too long to get someone to the mountain to help?*

Cornwallis was back at his post. Parker leaned on a tree, watching the dog. Each minute that passed felt like an hour.

Cornwallis stood and started barking at the empty space beyond the cliff.

Parker crouched. "What is it, boy? What is it?"

The dog turned and barked at the woods. Esther began scanning the dense forest for signs of an animal. Every sense heightened. She heard something in the distance.

"Quiet, Cornwallis," she said. He kept barking.

"Cornwallis," Parker said in a commanding tone. "Silence." And the brilliant dog obeyed.

They both listened. She asked, "Is that a motor? On the trail?" Another sound. She turned to the cliff and walked as close as she dared. "Parker! A helicopter!"

He joined her and they scanned the western horizon while the sound grew. From the north, an orange and white coast guard helicopter raced toward the cliffs. It swung around and hovered at eye level. The pilot waved. They jumped up and down, waving back.

The helicopter climbed higher in the sky, and Parker yelled over the noise, "They aren't leaving, are they?"

Another sound joined the copter—a distant siren—and then it was gone, drowned out by the copter.

The copter slowly turned until the nose faced north. The entire side was open. Parker and Esther could see a hoist with a man in a helmet and orange jumpsuit standing by, holding onto something inside.

Esther had lived in Necanicum long enough to know the man was a rescue diver. His job entailed jumping into the ocean to save boaters. Another man was on the seat by the hoist. They put a harness on the man standing, and he made motions at the pilot. The bird rose higher, until they couldn't see inside. It hovered closer to the cliffs.

The wind caused by the rotors dislodged gravel and debris. Esther shaded her eyes and worried about what was falling on Paisley.

Then a man on a cable leapt out of the copter and began descending, closer and closer.

"He's too far out!" Parker shouted. "They'll hit the trees before he reaches her!"

Esther knew they had done this before. Every year of her life, one or two hikers tried to scale the cliffs only to have to call for a rescue. She found herself praying silently.

The helicopter climbed again, pulling the rescue diver up. He swung unexpectedly toward the trees. They saw the hoist operator lean out of the door, watching him.

The hoist operator continued to lower the rescue diver until Esther couldn't see him anymore. She didn't dare get closer to the edge to watch. Parker still held Cornwallis as he watched the cable begin moving, in and out like he was swinging. Then it stopped.

Like magic, the noise continued while the pilot held everything still. The cable swung out and the bird lifted away from the trees. Paisley was in the harness clinging to the rescue diver, her head buried.

Parker caught sight of her and raised both arms in a cheer, letting go of Cornwallis. He swept Esther up in a hug and kissed her on the cheek, squeezing her so tightly she couldn't do anything but laugh with joy.

They watched as Paisley was taken into the helicopter. One of the coast guard waved out the open door. The helicopter dropped down and flew away, leaving them holding each other. They waved and Cornwallis barked at the cliff's edge.

"Guys! Guys!" Sophie was yelling again. "Did they get her?" She came running toward Esther with a massive grin on her face. Nephi followed, shirtless.

"Where's your shirt?" Esther asked.

"I marked the trail." He handed her back her headband.

"Whose idea was it to use your whole shirt?" she asked skeptically while putting her hair back up.

"Mine." Sophie grinned proudly. She slapped Nephi's hard abs and winked at Esther.

"Seriously?" Esther said.

"Where do you think they've taken her?" Parker strapped on his sister's pink hydro-pack.

"Probably Necanicum Hospital. It's the closest. Depending on her injuries. They could take her into Portland to a trauma unit if her injuries are worse than they looked to me." Esther realized she had learned a lot listening to her mother on the crisis line.

"Let's go find her again." Nephi took off running without waiting for an answer.

# 31

# One Day You'll Thank Me

A quad met them at the spot marked by Nephi's shirt. Mr. Brown, the Oceanside High basketball coach was driving it, and a deputy was his passenger. It pulled a small trailer.

The deputy said, "Hey, we were gathering the high angle volunteer team when the coast guard said it wasn't safe. They were going to get your hiker. Did they get her?"

"They did," Parker said. "Do you know where they've taken her? It's my sister."

"Necanicum Hospital. The chief is calling your parents so they can meet her there. We came up to give you a lift down, and well, because we love driving the quad."

The deputy rearranged the equipment so they could get on the trailer. Esther, Parker, and Sophie sat down. The deputy looked Nephi's tall frame up and down. Then he looked at the trailer. He shook his head and started to try to make more room for Nephi.

"I'll run," Nephi offered.

The deputy let out a sigh of relief. Sophie perched on top of a toolbox, while Esther and Parker's feet hung off the back.

"That looks painful." The deputy examined Esther's knee. She looked down and realized dried blood and dirt were packed in her kneecap. Blood had dried on her leg and pooled in her shoe.

The deputy knelt and looked closer at the injury. "We have an ambulance standing by. Do you want a ride to the hospital? You need to get the dirt and rocks cleaned out of your wound."

"No. Nephi can take me in his truck when we get to the parking lot." She wasn't ready to leave her friends.

The ride down the mountain in the little trailer was slow but better than on foot. Nephi easily kept up with them.

While they were en route the deputy touched his earpiece and said, "Copy." He stopped driving for a moment, turned, and told them, "Paisley is at Necanicum, safe and sound. Your parents are on their way."

"Let's go!" Parker said.

He was beaming. Esther would have hugged him if she hadn't been hanging on for dear life.

When they left the gravel trail and pulled into the parking lot, they stopped by an idling ambulance. A medic and the driver got out, walked over, and looked at her knee.

"Does it hurt?" the medic asked.

"Not at all. I can get myself to the clinic or the hospital to have it looked at."

He nodded, smiled, and left her to take care of her injury.

Esther stood up and then immediately sat back down and held her breath. Somewhere on the way down the mountain, the adrenaline had left her body and her knee began to burn like it was on fire. She didn't want to put her weight on it.

Parker noticed and immediately put his arm around her back and said, "Here, let me help you. Let's get you to the truck."

Nephi saw what was happening and sprinted ahead to open the passenger door for her. Sophie sat in the middle, Esther took shotgun, and Parker rode in the back while Nephi drove to the hospital.

# 32

# Just What the Doctor Ordered

Parker left them in the parking lot and ran to the emergency room to find Paisley. Nephi helped Esther limp slowly to the nurse's station, where they were asked to wait. Thirty minutes passed so slowly that it felt more like two hours.

Sophie was on her phone. "No, Mom, I wasn't in any danger. We were just on a morning hike when we found her. Uh huh. Yes. I will practice the violin twice tomorrow. No, I didn't feed the fish. Yes. I'm going to make sure Esther gets home okay. I have my cell phone if you need me, but the battery is almost dead, so I better go."

Esther said, "I guess I should call Mom and face the music."

"It isn't your mom I'm worried about. It's your new stepdad I wonder about," Nephi said. "What if he's as tough at home as he is in uniform? I'm sure he's heard what was going on."

"Maybe I'll text her." Esther texted her mother on Sophie's phone. She explained that Paisley had been found. She was at the hospital with Parker to see Paisley. Also, when she was with Parker's dog, she had cut her knee up. She was going to have it looked at in the emergency room. But it wasn't serious, and she would be home soon. Nephi was with her and would drive her home.

Nephi was looking over her shoulder. "Nice," was his only comment.

It wasn't long before the nurse brought them back to the main area in the small emergency room. There was a nurse's station in the center and four beds surrounding it, separated by curtains.

They put her in one of the beds. She realized Paisley was in the next bed, on the other side of the curtain.

She could see Parker's legs under the curtain and hear his family talking to Paisley in low tones. There were moments of silence when the nurse appeared to be doing something. It was hard to tell by the feet moving around the hospital bed what was going on.

Nephi sat in a chair by her bed. Sophie stood close to the sheet, listening to Paisley's family. The bed was tipped up, allowing her to sit up and lean against it. There was a thin pillow behind her head. As she relaxed she realized how tired she was. But she couldn't close her eyes. All she could do was listen in fascination to the happy reunion in the bed next to hers. She began to want her mom.

She texted her mother, "You can come up if you want, but I won't be here long."

Her mother replied, "At Mary's soccer game in Wheelton. Leaving now. On our away. Send pics. So sorry you got hurt! I hope it doesn't keep you from track. I bet you love running."

*Not being able to run long distance track is the silver lining to this entire thing,* Esther thought. For a split second she worried about her grades and the extra credit.

The nurse came in with a bucket and a tray of tools. She put a pad under Esther's knee. Esther's eyes widened when she looked closer at the tweezers and other instruments of torture on the metal rolling tray. The nurse began washing dirt out of her wound using a saline solution.

Esther sucked her breath in and held it, clutching at the bed sheets with both hands and closing her eyes. Sophie looked up from her phone, her eyebrows raising. She turned slightly green and quickly looked back down at her cell.

"This is going to sting a little," the nurse said without looking up. Esther decided the woman was the queen of understatement. She tried to think about anything else but what was happening with her knee.

"How are we coming along?" a man's voice asked, interrupting her thoughts. Esther peeked out of one eye and saw a doctor in a long white coat.

After introducing himself as Dr. Kelly, he looked over the nurse's shoulder while he pulled on gloves and put a mask over his face. The nurse stood up and stepped back. He motioned to the nurse, who must have read his mind and brought a lens with a light to Esther's bedside.

The doctor looked through the magnifying glass and examined her wound with gloved hands. "I don't think we need to, or even can, stitch it. I don't think you've broken anything. But you should stay off of it for a few days and give this wound time to start the healing process."

"Will you give me a note to excuse me from PE and track?" she asked.

Sophie actually snorted. "Hey, no fair!" she said.

"Of course. Nurse?" The doctor led the nurse outside the curtain. He gave her a series of directions and threw away his gloves.

A few moments later, Esther heard the doctor's voice again on the other side of the curtain, speaking to Paisley.

The doctor said, "You are one lucky lady. You were dehydrated, so we've given you IV fluids. The fracture on your ankle didn't do any serious damage and should heal nicely. We are going to put you in a boot until the swelling is under control. The nurse will set you up with an orthopedist before you leave."

Paisley's mother asked, "What about her face?"

"It's a bad sunburn. We can give you some burn cream for comfort. My guess is she is going to peel, and the swelling should go down in the next day or so. Don't pop the little blisters. Let it heal naturally. Watch for signs of infection. I'll write a prescription for pain if it will help you sleep. Sleep is important and we don't want the pain to keep her awake."

Esther could hear the doctor tell the nurse what he wanted before he left.

# 33

# Old Friends and New

It got quiet again, while the nurse used the magnifying glass to dig gravel out of Esther's knee. Sophie stood up and made her way around the bed to the curtain and stood near Parker's feet.

"Parker," Sophie whispered and poked him through the curtain.

"Sophie!" Esther hissed.

Nephi snickered and said in his deepest voice, "Parker, this is your conscience. You've been a bad boy."

"Nephi!" Esther scolded, appalled.

Parker ripped the curtain back, smiling from ear to ear, and Nephi bumped Paisley's bed, trying to get to him. They hugged and slapped each other on the back. Paisley reached for Nephi, without talking, tears running down her swollen face. He hugged her.

"You stink," she said in a raspy voice. She pushed him away, laughing weakly.

Parker put an arm around Esther, almost pulling her off the bed. He drew Sophie into a group hug. A muffled voice between them said, "She's right. You boys stink!" Micro fists pushed them apart and they moved until Esther buried her face in his neck.

"All right," the nurse said. "Hold still!" The joyful reunion continued. Parker was telling his father how they found Paisley when her nurse interrupted so she could fit Paisley's ankle with a black boot.

While the nurse worked quickly, the chief entered the emergency room.

"Hello, folks. Paisley," the chief began. "There are about thirty thousand fans who will be glad to hear you're alive. Hopefully they'll stop calling my station."

Paisley said softly, "I'm done with social media for a while." She tried to smile, but her lips were too chapped.

"We need to talk, young lady," the chief continued. He asked Mr. Stuart and the nurse, "How much longer do you think she will be here?"

"As soon as they sign," the nurse said. "The doctor says she's good to go." The nurse removed her IV, bandaged her arm, and left for a moment.

"Can we use the room?" the chief asked the nurse. "This can't wait."

"She is so tired," her mother protested weakly. "Can you wait until we get her cleaned up and a little food in her? Say, after dinner?"

"I'm afraid not. This is important, ma'am. I need to ask her some questions before she leaves the hospital. Could you step out?"

Mrs. Stuart's chin pulled in and her mouth fell open. "Excuse me?" She stood and got between her daughter and the chief. Mr. Stuart stood on the other side of the bed and the room became quiet.

The chief took his hat off. "Ma'am, there are some things she might be more comfortable discussing without her parents."

"I don't understand," Mrs. Stuart snapped.

The chief shifted from one foot to another and kept looking down and playing with his hat. "Well, it's like this. I have a sexual assault advocate in the lobby if she's needed."

Paisley sat straight up in bed and began waving her hands. She said in a raspy voice, "It's okay. I don't need her." A smile made her lips crack and she winced but chuckled. "Cornwallis took care of me." She fell back into the bed. Talking seemed to take effort.

The chief, who must have been holding his breath, said, "Phew. Well, I'm glad to hear that."

Paisley's mother sat down hard in a plastic chair. She looked at her daughter with her eyebrows raised and her mouth open. She reached out and took Paisley's hand and said, "Oh, thank heavens."

Mr. Stuart's eyes filled with tears, and he sniffed as he bent over and kissed his little girl on the head. He turned his head and stood against the wall.

A jolt went through Esther. She knew what her mother did for work and how cruel the world could be. All she had been thinking about was being a hero and getting Paisley off the mountain, herself, and her knee. She had never realized how close Paisley was to being hurt in a way so many girls were, something almost worse than losing your life.

"Well," the chief said, "that does make this a little easier."

Esther studied his aviator glasses and handlebar mustache for any sign of a smile. Nothing.

"I still need to ask a few questions for my report so we know how to proceed."

# 34

# Make a Long Story Short

Paisley sat up again, this time with all the poise Esther was familiar with. She said, "They can stay."

"Your parents?" the chief asked.

"And my friends." She waved her hand, indicating everyone in the room.

Sophie held her phone up. "Do you want me to videotape the interview?"

Paisley actually laughed. "No, but come here." She held out her hand for Sophie's phone.

"Now, I need to get this done," the chief said. Paisley ignored him.

"Come on, Esther," Paisley said. Esther looked at the nurse, who shrugged and let her hop over to the bed.

"Chief?" Paisley said, "would you take our picture?"

"Oh, good grief. Now this is no joke, young lady."

For the first time, Esther saw what people loved about Paisley. She made them all feel wanted.

"Oh come on now, Chief. I'll take one with you next," she quipped.

The chief jammed his hat back on his head and reluctantly took the cell phone. They all squeezed in.

The chief held the phone up, looked irritated, and said gruffly, "Say cheese."

They all leaned in and Paisley held up her hands in peace signs. Esther regretted all the times she had judged Paisley.

"I survived!" Paisley hugged her twin. "Okay, Chief. Let's get on with it."

The chief shook his head. "You're one tough little lady."

"Whoa, Chief," Sophie said, "don't go getting soft on us."

The chief pulled out his little leather note pad and recorder. "Can I record this?"

"Sure. If you have to." Paisley smiled, winced, and touched her chapped lips.

"You're still a minor. I need your parents' permission."

After he had permission, the chief stated all the names in the room and asked for everyone's date of birth and contact information.

"Paisley," the chief said. "I need to get the details of what happened on the mountain. We know that Herbert Anderson is dead. We have confirmation that a body found on the beach last night belonged to him. Can you tell us what happened in your own words? You're not in trouble."

Esther looked around and was sure, if it was her, she couldn't talk in front of a group like this. Paisley, however, seemed to gain strength from her brother as well as everyone else in the room.

Paisley took a sip of water. "I was running at night with Cornwallis. I've done it a hundred times and never had a problem. But Friday was a rough day, and I wasn't really paying attention. I got to the trailhead and turned around. I didn't plan on running the trail at night."

She took another sip and went on. "But car lights blinded me. I stopped to yell at the driver, but it was Herbert. I've only met him a few times, but I knew he's a total creeper. Cornwallis was on a leash or I think he would have eaten him alive."

"That dog is our hero," Parker offered.

"Right?" Paisley reached out to hold Parker's hand. "But he said something. At first I couldn't hear him. Then I realized he was saying he had a gun. He thought I owed him something, even though I didn't even know him, and I needed to understand that we were meant to be together. I didn't know what to do. He got out of the car pointed a gun at me."

She was silent for a moment, and Esther realized Paisley was replaying the memories in her mind. Her eyes moved but she wasn't looking at anything or anyone. After a minute she adjusted herself on the bed and went on.

"This woman had come to our school this year—Grace. She did a short class on self-defense with a guy and then told us if we wanted to live the best thing to do was fight."

Esther had taken the class Paisley was talking about. But because her mom taught it, she didn't really pay attention. She felt like she had heard it all before. In fact her mother was always talking about how to stay safe. She thought, *I should have listened. Mom was right.*

"So I knew I had to fight back. But Grace also told this story about when she told a guy that was trying to hurt her she would go with him, until she got somewhere she could scream for help. You know? She outsmarted him. So I told him he was right. I did like him. He had me at gunpoint, so I thought I needed to keep him happy until he let his guard down. He made me hike to the bunker."

She actually chuckled softly. "He was slow. If I had a clear shot or open space, I probably could have outrun him, but the trail is straight up.

"When we got to the bunker . . . He had a flashlight. It made it hard because he kept shining it in my face. But I realized if I could get outside the light, it was so dark in there he couldn't see me. I didn't know how big the room was, but it echoed. So when he was trying to pull my pack off, I slipped out of it and ran for it. I was up and out of the bunker before he knew what was happening, but Cornwallis barked, giving away our location. I tried hiding, but as soon as he was out, Cornwallis was pulling on the leash, so I let go . . . "

She sat for a minute, remembering. *Paisley will have post-traumatic stress disorder like I do. I know that feeling of getting lost in a memory.*

The chief looked up from his notes. "Go on," he said.

Paisley's eyes were open, but she was back on the mountain. "Cornwallis was like I had never seen him before. He went for his throat. The gun went off and I stayed behind a tree. I couldn't look. Then the man was screaming, and Cornwallis was whining, so I looked.

"The man must have stepped off the cliff. It was like the mountain was falling apart. It kept losing ground and he was trying to climb back up. He was holding onto anything he could grab and Cornwallis's leash. The leash was the only thing keeping him alive.

"Then Cornwallis just put his neck out and the leash slipped over his head. The fern gave way and the man was gone. I ran to the edge. I don't know why . . . "

She closed her eyes. "It gave way. I was falling and Cornwallis was rolling. It stopped and I was laying on loose gravel and dirt. We were there for a long time."

"How long?" the chief asked.

"The sun rose. I had hurt my left ankle or leg. It was hard to stand still, but at least I had stopped sliding. Cornwallis just whimpered. I could see the top of the cliff. It was so close, but I couldn't let go of him. Cornwallis had saved my life. So I waited, hoping someone would come looking for us."

Her mother let out a small groan. Esther knew Melissa hadn't even known Paisley was missing when she was hanging on for her life.

"I remember the heat, the rain, trying to catch raindrops and the water making the hill slide away right next to us. My right leg was getting so tired. When no one came, I decided I had to try. I don't know what time it was when I pushed Cornwallis up, and thought at least I could save him. I got him to the edge. He started scrambling, and it brought the whole mountain down on me.

"I don't know how, I just started grabbing for anything. Then my right foot hit a rock and I let the rest of the mountain fall around me. That's where you found me."

"Holy crepes!" Sophie said. "You should be dead!"

"Yeah," Paisley said. "Don't think I'm crazy, but I started falling asleep. I would have fallen, but I could swear I heard Parker calling me even though he wasn't there. I must have been dreaming." Her voice broke, and the tears finally started coming.

Parker climbed up on the bed and held her. Esther cried, Sophie sniffed loudly, and Nephi held his breath.

The chief nodded at her parents, put away his recorder and note pad, and quietly left them.

# 35

# Facing the Music

The nurse got Esther and Paisley ready to check out. Esther knew it was time to go home and face the music. She'd broken a thousand rules, and yet, everything she had done felt right.

As Paisley got into a wheelchair to leave she said, "Everybody come over tonight. I don't want to be alone. Not today."

"They can join us for dinner," Parker's mother offered, sounding kind but firm.

Paisley's father signed her out. Parker gave Esther a quick hug and waved good-bye before he joined his family. Mr. Stuart pushed Paisley in a wheelchair to their waiting car.

"I guess we go back to school and the world goes on. Do you think Parker and Paisley will hang out with us at school?" Sophie asked. "Many relationships forged in crisis don't last."

Sophie's statement hung heavy in the air. Nephi glanced up from his phone and watched the Stuarts pull out of the parking lot. Esther sat silently, wondering about Parker, school, and how much she had changed in just a few days. Would things with Parker go back to the way they were when they went back to school?

✦ ✦ ✦

Esther's mother pulled up to the house at the same time they arrived. Sophie excused herself. She ran home to shower, change into her own clothes, and feed the dog.

"Coward!" Esther called to her retreating form.

Grace took Mary into the house ahead of them.

Nephi came around to her car door and handed her the crutches the hospital had given her. He helped her hop to the stairs. When she stopped at the bottom, he scooped her up, grunting like she weighed a thousand pounds and made a show of carrying her into the living room.

"See ya," he said. "I gotta try to get even more handsome for Paisley." With that he smirked and added, "But we all know it's not possible." He flexed his arms and left her alone with her mother.

Grace sent Mary upstairs to change out of her soccer gear and to shower. Then, she sat on the coffee table and looked at Esther's knee with a look that was a cross between concern and disgust. Esther braced herself for the verbal barrage that she was sure she deserved.

Miss Molly came down the stairs and jumped in Esther's lap. She felt wonderful. Esther held her and stroked her soft fur until she purred loudly.

"Esther," her mom said and looked her in the eyes. "You're sixteen. You're almost an adult. I want to let you be as independent as you want to be, but I need to be able to trust your judgment."

Esther had to look away from her mother's eyes. "I'm sorry, Mom."

"Sorry about what?"

"I haven't been very honest." She started picking at the edge of the bandage on her leg. She waited for her mom to yell at her, ground her, something. But her mother was quiet.

She searched her mother's concerned face. She wanted to tell her everything.

"Mom? Do you think God will punish me? Did I get hurt because I lied?"

"What makes you think that?"

A picture of the red couch flashed in her mind. "Everything. The Bible. My Sunday School teachers who tell us if we're good and keep all the commandments we will be safe and prosper."

"So, you feel like you have to be perfect to be loved by God?" her mother asked.

"Yes. Well . . . bad things happen when I'm not good," she said softly.

"What bad things, sweetheart?"

The question made Esther think. She could hear her little sister singing while she showered upstairs. A part of her wished her little sister would call their mom and the conversation would end.

But another part of her had to know, wanted to understand if the fear she had carried with her or all of her life was real. She finally decided to ask. She took in a deep breath and let it out, looking her mother at the face.

"Sometimes if I'm not perfect I'm afraid terrible things will happen like when I made my father so mad he cut you." The words came out of Esther in a rush.

Her mother's eyebrows knit, and she tilted her head and asked, "You mean the last day we lived at the brick house? The day he was arrested?"

Esther nodded silently.

"Oh, honey, no!" Her mother's eyes opened wide, and her brows rose. "Did you think that was your fault? You were only eight years old."

A single tear tickled down Esther's cheek. She held her breath and nodded.

"No, no, no. It wasn't either of our fault. It was your father who made the choice to do what he did."

Esther shook her head back and forth. "No, Mom. I wouldn't stop crying. I was throwing a tantrum. You had to throw me behind the couch. And it was all over a pile of stupid blocks!"

Her mother thought for a moment. She reached out and wiped the tear from Esther's cheek. Miss Molly looked at her with concern.

She said, "There are children all over the world who throw tantrums. No one dies and their families don't end. Just think about your little sister."

"Mary does throw some huge fits." Esther laughed nervously.

"And I haven't tried to kill anyone. Why?"

Esther knew the answer. "Because you aren't like he was, abusive."

Her mom nodded. "Did you know there are lots of people in the world that experience bad things and blame themselves like you do?"

"No," Esther said hesitantly.

"Well, there are. You see, we can't stand the thought of the world being as out of control as it is. Bad things happen to good people like Paisley, and so we look for a reason, something we can control. But there is only one thing we truly have control over, and that's our choices. So, sometimes we get a silly notion that it must be our fault. Because if it's our fault, then at least we can do something to change it or control it. Do you understand?"

Esther was having a hard time keeping up. Every new idea was making her rethink everything she knew. She shook her head. "I don't know. No, not really."

"Well, take a look at Paisley. She isn't perfect, but was there anything she did to cause this bad thing to happen to her?"

"She was on social media?" Ether offered.

"Millions of young people are on social media and nothing bad happens to them," her mom said.

"Well, she's pretty?" Esther tried again to find a way to explain what had happened.

"Ah," her mother smiled. "We call that victim blaming. Should every pretty or even every pretty and mean girl be hurt like Paisley was?"

Esther realized the absurdity of the idea. And then the same thought that always wandered through her mind was back again.

"Mom? How can God love me or even want me if I lie to you or I'm not perfect, though?" she asked earnestly.

"Did God love the lepers, the blind, and all the people he healed?"

"I guess so."

"Esther, I know it's a lot to take in, but He loves you where you are, and that's all you need to know today. But I want you to remember one more really important thing."

"What's that?" Esther asked.

"You get to be human. You aren't going to be punished for learning and growing up. People get to make choices. The person that hurt Paisley is responsible for his bad choices, not God, and certainly not Paisley. God kept you alive today and brought you back to me."

Her mother gathered her up in a big hug and whispered in her ear, "It's not your fault. It was never your fault."

New tears fell when Esther heard the words she'd wanted to hear, needed to hear. "Does that mean I'm not grounded?" Esther asked.

"I didn't say that!" her mother answered, laughing.

Esther laughed and wiped the tears from her eyes.

Her mother gave her a quick hug and said, "I promised Mary I would make cookies tonight. But first I have to make dinner. Do you want to come in the kitchen with me?"

"I would, but we are invited to go to the Stuarts in a few hours. Can you help me, Mom? I would really like to wash my hair, and I can't get my knee wet."

"Sure, if you promise to serenade me like your sister."

The front door opened. Hart stood in the open door in his police uniform. Molly hissed and ran up the stairs.

His eyes were moist, and his mouth was in a firm line. He took his hat off and held it, standing just inside the door across the room from them.

Esther realized his hands were shaking. She pushed herself up onto one foot, balancing on the arm of the sofa.

The room was silent. He swallowed hard and looked in Esther's eyes. "I was so scared." He had to stop to compose himself. "I know I'm not your actual father, but . . . I was hearing it all on the scanner. The chief just filled me in. I was supposed to be working but . . . " He closed his eyes.

Then, he closed the distance between them, wrapping her in his arms. He smelled of fear and aftershave. His bulletproof vest was hard, and his badge was pressed into her forehead. He held her close to his heart and she melted. Her tears joined his. Trying to trust and take it in, she thought, *This—this is what it's like to be loved by a father.*

# 36

## Home Sweet Home

Esther and Parker crossed the back lawn of the Stuarts' house to the gazebo. All the twinkle lights were on in the trees and around tables.

Wicker chairs and tables with pizza, popcorn, and soda pop filled the gazebo.

Nephi and Sophie were lighting a gas fireplace in the center of the gathering.

Paisley was on a chaise lounge. Cornwallis sat next to her with his head in her lap, her protector. The dog looked up when Esther sat nearby, but must have approved because he laid down on the cement and yawned.

"Are you sure you're not too tired for this?" Esther asked.

"No. I had a nap. And besides," she said, "I feel like life is just a little more precious than it was before."

Although she was still sunburned, her hair was perfect again. Even her leisure sweats were stylish. But Esther didn't feel envy. She appreciated Paisley's resilience and had a newfound respect for her new friend.

"So, Paisley," Sophie said as she sat by her. "You need a social media manager and a security system. I'm your girl."

Paisley laughed. "I thought I had it all handled," she said, looking at Parker. "Bridget and I called the crisis line when Herbert kept messaging me. They said if he was stalking me, the first step was to tell him I didn't want any more contact and then write down the date. So I did. I didn't see him again until the other night." She shrugged.

Parker leaned toward his sister and said, "It isn't your fault." The very thing Esther's mother had just told her, the thing she had longed to hear for years. She felt her heart burn when she looked at him. She watched Paisley take it in and smile at her twin brother.

"Hey, sis. Why aren't you grounded?" Parker asked.

"Why aren't you?" She smiled.

"I could stand to be grounded here." Nephi stuffed his mouth full of pizza.

"I have a question," Paisley said. "I had a lot of time on that mountain to think about what mattered and about how I have been living. I realized how important my family was to me and that maybe I should choose friends for more reasons than how they look in photos."

"Finally! Let's hear it. Come on," Parker said.

"You were right," Paisley offered. "You warned me, and I didn't listen. But I can see now that you have found some pretty great peeps to hang with. So, I wondered . . . would you . . . all of you, go to prom with me?"

"Yes!" Nephi jumped up and did his touchdown dance, arms in the air making the signs for victory.

"Wait," Parker said. "What if I wanted to take Esther?"

Esther's eyes grew wide and a shiver ran up her spine. "Me?"

"I was thinking we could go as a group. You know? Dance together, hang together," Paisley insisted.

Sophie said, "Great. But, Esther, you have to save a dance with me. I'm done holding up the wall and guzzling the punch alone."

"I'll be bringing one more guest." Paisley gave a sly smile.

"Who?" Nephi asked. He sat down, tilted his head and waited for the bad news.

"Not Bridget!" Parker's eyes got big and he shook his head, grimacing.

Paisley laughed a hearty laugh. "No. Not Bridget."

"Okay, then. I'm in." Parker laughed.

"Me too," Esther said. "This way I won't have to buy Sophie flowers and dance with my uncle." She smiled and gave Nephi a friendly push. "Seriously. Who is it? Is it someone from Oceanside High?"

A house door opened, and Parker's parents crossed the lawn to join them.

"Anyone for s'mores?" his dad asked. He had roasting sticks and a bag of marshmallows and chocolate. Mrs. Stuart put the graham crackers on a table by the fireplace and pulled up a chair.

"Sorry I kept you from work, Dad," Paisley offered.

"There will be a lot less of that." Her dad opened the package of marshmallows and put one on a roaster.

"Oh no! Did something happen?" Paisley asked. Her dry face gathered in concern.

"Yes," he said. "I had my priorities reorganized and have a second chance to spend more time with my family. I quit today. I am going to work in a clinic as a family practitioner, but I am never going to let it consume me again."

"Wait!" Sophie said. "What about our tree house? Will you go back to England? Are you moving?"

He laughed. "I think we can afford to stay here."

Paisley smiled. "I just want you to be happy, Father."

Her dad beamed. "Oh, I am my beautiful girl. Nothing in the world could make me sad tonight."

# 37
# Prom by the Beach

Esther, Sophie, and Nephi received embossed notes not long after. The invitations were for the day of prom. They were to meet in a nearby town's expensive spa and salon, Namaste.

The instructions had been clear. They were to each text Paisley their sizes, measurements, favorite colors, foods, and allergies. They were to arrive no later than ten in the morning at Namaste on the day of prom. And they were to wear nothing but shorts, a shirt, and flip flops.

"No way!" Sophie said. "I hate surprises. I'm calling the spa. No. I am going over there for the cheapest pedicure they have."

Esther laughed so hard she snorted, "Sophie! Have you looked at her photos? Who do you want getting you ready for prom? Me and Grandma Mable, or Paisley?"

"Fine. What does Nephi think?"

"He thought it meant he didn't need to buy flowers. So cheap. I saved him from that blooper." Esther chuckled. "I asked Parker what we should contribute to the spa or dinner costs. I have a little savings account and it felt right."

"What did he say?"

"He said no one could pay for a single thing. So, I told him you and I would do dessert after the prom. He asked where and I told him he had his surprises and we had ours.

"So what are we going to do?" Sophie asked.

"I have absolutely no idea."

"How big is that savings account?"

"Twelve dollars and thirty five cents."

"We're doomed."

✦ ✦ ✦

Esther got up early on the Saturday of prom. She spent two hours doing her hair and makeup while Hope slept like a baby and Nephi snored on the living room couch. She thought it was probably silly, but she was terrified.

*Someone is going to tell him I have never been to a dance other than in the church gymnasium. I've only danced with Nephi, who stepped on my feet with his size-fourteen shoes.*

At nine thirty Sophie knocked on the front door. Esther's sister, Mary, answered it. She opened the door and said, "It's Soapy eats!" and slammed it in Sophie's face.

Sophie let her self in. "Thanks, Fairy Mary."

"Mom! She called me a fairy."

Esther's mom called from the kitchen, "I thought you liked fairies?"

Mary looked confused for a moment, "Wait! I do! I need my wings!" She ran for the stairs and her extensive costume collection.

"Hey, Sophie," Esther said.

"Nice hair! Why did you straighten it if we're getting it styled?" Sophie walked around her while Esther shrugged.

"I took Mom's flat iron to it."

"Did you iron your T-shirt? Did you wash your flip flops?"

"Yeah."

Nephi called from the breakfast table in the kitchen, "Don't be nervous."

"You should be more nervous," Esther called back to him.

Grandma Mable came out of the kitchen and smiled at her. "Parker is lucky to be your friend. Stand by the fireplace and let me take your picture. Nephi! Stop eating and get out here."

"Mom! No one needs a picture to remember how handsome I am. Just take the girls' picture."

"Nephi." Mable raised one eyebrow and waited. Nephi reluctantly joined the girls by the fireplace. He stood between them and puffed out his chest, striking a pose. He put one arm around Esther's shoulders and rested the other on Sophie's head.

"Hey, Sasquatch." Sophie playfully pushed his arm off her head. He picked her up like a baby, and Mable started snapping pictures while he laughed.

Hart came out of the kitchen to watch. "Tell Parker I said to have you home at a reasonable hour. And, Sophie, you might as well move in. You two are stuck together like glue."

"We're going to be late! Let's get this party started," Sophie said.

Namaste was twenty minutes down the coast in Cabot's Cove. To find it, they pulled off the highway onto a gravel road with a small sign that read "Namaste" and "Guests only." The turn was toward the ocean. The road circled around a small mountain. It looked like they were going to drive on the narrow road and right into the ocean.

Sophie and Esther leaned toward the mountain, willing Nephi's truck closer to the inside of the road. Esther realized she was holding her breath.

In a quarter mile, they rounded the west side of the mountain. Thankfully, the road opened onto a large gravel parking lot circled by old pine trees, twisted in pacific storms. Nephi parked the truck between a massive gold SUV and a long black limousine, one of two limousine's in the parking lot. The limo driver eyed him suspiciously as he leaned against his car reading a newspaper.

"I feel underdressed." Nephi looked at the girls and then down at his shorts and torn football jersey.

"You're my driver. I should buy you one of those cute limo driver outfits like his," Sophie said.

"Well, here goes nothing." Esther had butterflies in her stomach. But they were the good kind, the hopeful fluttering feelings that something magical was about to happen. It felt like Christmas Eve.

Hanging on the cliff was a one-story building that seemed to be as twisted as the pines. It wandered and hung on the edge. Through the front entryway they could see the infinity hot tub that hung and ran like a waterfall on the cliff's edge. Cedar deck chairs surrounded it. A woman in a fluffy white robe sat on one drinking something with celery in it and reading a magazine.

"Oh, no. I am not getting naked." Nephi's eyes were the size of pancakes, and he had a nervous half-smile on his face.

"If Paisley wears a robe too?" Esther asked.

"Get out of my way. Let's go." A grin replaced his nervous smile and he headed for the spa.

Paisley met them at the door with Parker. They both had on white robes and rubber Jerusalem sandals.

"Hi, guys! I'm so excited." She hugged them all. Nephi stood there while she hugged him, arms straight. Then he reached out, not sure of what to do with a girl in a robe, but she stepped back.

"Girls go that way." Parker pointed at a door to the right made of mirrored glass.

Then Parker pointed to a door that led to the other side of the building. "Mate, we go that way. Ransom is waiting for us in the sauna."

"Shut the front door!" Sophie said.

"Oh, I hope you don't mind," Paisley said. "I didn't want us to be an odd number. Would you mind dancing and going into dinner with Ransom, Sophie? If not, I can. I was hoping to dance with Nephi."

"Shut the front door!"

"You have got to come up with something more interesting to say before dinner." Esther laughed at Sophie's face. Her mouth was open, and her round glasses only made her shock look more comical.

Paisley laughed. "You know what I like about you, Sonoko Ito? Your absolute honesty. You are not only brilliant and beautiful, but you're honest and hilarious."

Sophie took off her glasses and handed them to Paisley. "Here, you need these more than I do."

Ransom came out of the men's locker room in a robe. "Paisley. Parker. Thanks for letting me tag along. This spa is great."

"Ransom," Paisley said, "this is Sophie. Sophie, Ransom."

Ransom flashed a white smile at Sophie. "Sophie. Do you like to dance? I hope you don't mind going with me."

Sophie's mouth was open. She didn't say a word. Esther poked her with her elbow.

"No, I don't mind, and I can dance. I usually take the lead with Esther, but I can let you lead."

✦ ✦ ✦

After Esther, Paisley, and Sophie passed through the glass doors to the women's side of the spa, the staff gave them large fluffy robes and sandals. Paisley had black one-piece bathing suits for them.

"Phew!" Sophie said. "I wondered what was under the robes."

Paisley laughed, her deep, contagious laugh. "Since the big pool is co-ed, the spa requests modesty. We have mani-pedis, hair appointments, facials, and professional makeup between one and five this afternoon. For now we can use the sauna, steam rooms, and the women's rain showers or the large infinity hot tub you saw when you came in.

Esther touched her straightened hair and smiled. *Waste of a good hairdo*, she thought. "Let's start in the pool," Esther said. "I have a hot tub at the house, but it is nothing like that pool. I almost wish my little sister could see it."

"Esther, I want to let you know what's been happening with my mom and dad." Paisley sat down and smiled at her.

"You don't have to," Esther said. "I know we all have bad days, and I can tell they love each other."

"But I want to tell you. I'm grateful in a strange way for what happened. Because of everything, my mother has really been struggling with the move, the loss of our horses, and, well, my parents weren't getting along as well as they usually do."

"It's okay." Esther interrupted her. "Really. No one's family is perfect. I am the best evidence of that."

Paisley smiled. "I guess that's true. It's just interesting how this good thing came out of such a bad thing. Normally, I wouldn't have anyone to talk to, so I appreciate you and Sophie. Because of everything that has happened both my parents are seeing counselors. They are even planning a trip together. I feel like a huge weight has lifted now that they have some support."

They changed and stored their things in lockers. Paisley led the way through the spa and back to the pool. It was surrounded by a large river rock patio, cedar patio chairs, and had a glass roof high above it all for rainy Oregon days. The pool bubbled and then seemed to fall over the cliff to the ocean several hundred feet below, but it actually went to a second garden terrace.

Esther looked out to the horizon. The sun was shining, and it was unusually warm. Sophie was applying copious amounts of sunscreen to her face and arms, but Esther marveled at the view.

*How does a small town girl like me, daughter of a man in prison, get to be so blessed? God, are you there? Do you love me?*

A warmth started in Esther's heart and spread to every part of her body. It was a sweet feeling that brought tears to her eyes and a slow smile.

"Are you okay?" Parker asked. He had walked up behind her.

"I am awesome," she answered.

"Yes, you are." He gave her a goofy grin. "Watch me make Paisley mad. Cannon ball!" He hit the pool and splashed Paisley and Sophie.

"Parker!"

Esther ran for the edge and yelled, "Cannon ball!" And with joy, she hit the water.

"I have never been treated like this," Sophie said.

"Really? It's about time, then." Paisley laughed easily.

They were walking together back to the locker room. Esther's makeup and hair were beautifully done.

"I will never look like this again." Esther caught a glimpse of herself in the mirror and studied her hair from the side.

"You have always looked like this," Paisley said.

"I don't think so," Sophie said. "I think there is a lot of lacquer on my eyelids and I really like it." Then she added, "I have been hiding for years behind sweaters, books, and thick glasses. I could get contacts, but I'm keeping the sweaters"

"Well, you can go back to your Clark Kent by day look if you want, but tonight, you're a superwoman." Paisley reached out and touched a gold thread woven into Sophie's hair. "Sophie, your hair is gorgeous. It is the healthiest, softest hair I have ever seen. And, Esther, I love your thick hair. You have flecks of gold woven in the brown and it's naturally wavy."

Sophie and Esther's geek girl ponytails were combed out. Sophie's hair was straight and long with a gold thread woven through it in random places. Esther's hair was curled in long beach waves.

When they got back to the locker room, the room had changed.

"It looks like a dress shop threw up in here," Sophie said. There was a rack of dresses and shoes, dresses hanging in random places, and shoes on the cedar bench in the middle of the stone floor. Three or four perfume bottles were organized on the counter.

Esther was stunned. "This is too much, Paisley."

"Most of these were mine, but I am a bit taller than Sophie, so the rest are on loan until we pick them out. My father said it was the least he could do for you, since you saved my life. I just wish I didn't still have to wear the boot tonight on my ankle."

Esther felt like a princess. She chose a long mint green gown with a beaded top and layers that would fly when she spun. She decided to wear her flip flops.

Sophie chose a completely gold beaded gown that fit curves Esther didn't know Sophie had. She wore four-inch platform shoes and was just over five feet tall.

Paisley stayed simple and black, with long white diamond studded gloves. Her shoes were one glass slipper to show off her red toenails and a black boot. She went with red lipstick, explaining she was over hot pink.

Together they walked to the door and joined the boys, who had turned into handsome men. Ransom's smoky eyes and dark hair was wavy. Nephi looked just like Nephi, and Parker had his ponytail. They all wore black tuxedos.

Parker hugged Esther and whispered in her ear, "I like you best in sweaters, but this is nice too. You're beautiful, always have been, inside and out."

Esther didn't know what to say. No one had ever talked to her like this before. "It's Paisley's things. And it took a whole spa to make my hair look like this."

"I liked you in the library. I liked you the first time I saw you. I love a girl with brains, and you were chewing a pencil over a calculous book when I came into the library. But no matter what I did, you wouldn't give me a second look," Parker said.

"Oh, I was looking. You just always had a fan club following you." Esther smiled.

"You did?"

"Honest."

Parker pushed a curl out of her face and smiled back at her. "And I bet Sophie had a running commentary going behind my back."

"That's why I love her. She says everything I wish I could. And when I doubt myself, she sets me straight," Esther said.

"I'm sure she does." Parker chuckled.

"Hey! I can hear you," Sophie said.

Ransom put his arm out to escort Sophie. "Thanks for allowing me to escort you to the dance tonight."

"Excuse me? This is the highlight of my life. I may never have a better night," Sophie told him. "So, thank you."

Ransom handed Sophie a rose corsage for her wrist and said, "I am so glad you're not taller than me. It is so hard to find a date that doesn't make me feel like I'm with my mother."

"How tall are you?" Sophie asked.

"Last I measured, I was five foot five inches. I constantly have to wear lifts in my shoes for movies."

"Wow, you're really tall," Sophie said. Esther hoped she would be a little less smitten as the night went on.

"And," Ransom said, "I hear you're brilliant. I am going to be going half days to online high school in the late summer and fall when we film. Would you consider tutoring me?"

"Shut the front door!" Sophie said.

Everyone laughed and Esther said, "We have got to teach you some manners, Miss Sophie."

"Wait," Sophie said, "what are you taking?"

"Advanced placement chemistry and English literature and composition."

"Shut the front door! Me too!"

Ransom led Sophie to the limousine. Parker held his arm out and walked with Esther. Nephi and Paisley were laughing at Sophie when Nephi picked up Paisley so her gown wouldn't get dirty in the gravel parking lot.

"Can we pick up the truck tomorrow?" Parker asked. "Ransom has offered to drive." A long limousine pulled up to the door.

"Okay, but don't forget, Esther and I planned the dessert," Sophie said.

"Soph! They won't want . . . "

"You people need to spend some time in our space," Sophie said. "You know, the everyday average-jane world. Desert after the dance."

When the DJ put on a slower song, Parker took Esther's right hand in his, put his arm around her waist, and danced like a prince in a movie.

Esther did her best to follow Parker's lead. At first she was nervous, and her palms were sweaty, but after a while she began to get the hang of it. For the first time in Esther's memory she was dancing with a boy instead of Sophie and Nephi.

Parker let go of her waist and twirled her while she laughed. "Good job! You missed both my feet." He grinned and pulled her closer.

The music changed and the beat picked up. This is where Esther was comfortable. Years of dance parties with Grandma Mable and Mary had prepared her. Parker, on the other hand, was at a total loss. He stiffly took a step to the right and then to the left while Esther danced around him and tried to teach him how to swing his hips. His hips were only made for waltzing, but he was still laughing and on the dance floor.

When the next song came on, Esther searched for Sophie. She wasn't dancing. She leaned close to Parker and said in his ear over the loud music, "Let's look for Sophie and Ransom. I could use some punch or water."

"Good idea." Parker took Esther's hand and led her off the dance floor. They made their way through the maze of people and were almost to the refreshment table when Esther spotted Sophie. She was at one of the tables alone. She had her elbows on the table and held her face up with her right hand while her left hand's fingers drummed on the table.

"Oh no," Esther said. "There's Sophie. Where's Ransom?"

"Over there." Parker pointed to the edge of the dance floor. Ransom was dancing with two girls from the freshman class.

"Oh no!" Esther let go of Parker's hand and wove through dancing teenagers jumping to loud, rhythmic music.

"Esther, wait." Parker caught up to her. "Ransom had better be good to her, or I will give him a piece of my mind."

Esther tipped her head. "Protective. I like it." They closed the distance to Sophie's table together.

"Sophie?" Esther watched Ransom get mobbed by another group of girls. "Don't you think it's time for dessert?"

"It was time to leave an hour ago," Sophie said.

Esther walked toward the dance floor with Parker on her heels.

"Ransom," Esther called. "Ransom!"

"What?" he called over the noise of the music and people.

"Are you ready for our desert?" she yelled.

"Am I!" Ransom stopped dancing. "Sorry, darlings. I've got to go," he said to the girls. They moved in closer, surrounding him, but he pushed his way through and ran to Sophie's table.

Leaning over, he shouted in Sophie's ear, "Do you want to get out of here?"

"Can we leave yesterday?" Sophie said.

Ransom grabbed her hand and ran for the door, a group of girls following him.

Parker and Esther rounded up Paisley and Nephi. They found them near the dance floor laughing hysterically over Nephi's unsuccessful attempt to moon walk.

"Nice dance skills!" Parker said and slapped Nephi on the back.

"Mom taught me." Parker grinned and Paisley laughed so hard she snorted.

"We're ready for desert. Are you?" Esther asked.

"When am I not ready for food?" Nephi took Paisley's hand and walked ahead of Esther and Parker clearing a path through the people.

They piled back into the limo with Ransom and Sophie.

After opening the electric window, the driver asked, "Where to?"

"My house," Esther said.

# 38
# BFFs

Esther and Sophie ran in the house and came back with Esther's little sister Mary's wagon. It was full of blankets and folding beach chairs.

"Now what do we do?" Parker asked.

"You trust us, and we walk." Esther shrugged and smiled.

Sophie started taking her shoes off and said, "After I take off these heels and get my flip flops on."

"Where are we going?" Nephi asked.

"It's a surprise." Esther winked at him.

Esther and Sophie led the group up the sidewalk and onto the beach.

"This is great." Parker fell into step with Esther.

"It's a beautiful night. We lucked out. No rain or wind, and look at the sky." Esther pointed up into the black night. The street lamps couldn't outshine the stars that blanketed the sky over the ocean. The clean smell of pine trees and the salty fishy smell of the ocean were her favorite.

Suddenly, Parker pulled her by the hand back behind the group. He stepped off the sidewalk and into the dark trees.

"Parker?" Esther started to say. And then it happened. A sweet kiss. Her first kiss. She thought her heart would burst. She felt it all the way down to her toes. Just as fast as he had pulled her off the sidewalk, he pulled her back to the sidewalk.

"We better hurry so we can catch up to the others," Parker said. He smiled at her and they walked a little faster.

She had no words. She wanted this moment to last forever. She realized she was smiling. She looked up at his blond hair, his handsome face, and knew what she liked best about him was on the inside. Everything she ever thought about herself, about Parker, and about Paisley was wrong, and she was so glad it was.

They fell into step with the group and passed the dunes and the seagrass, still pulling the wagon.

Just around the bend, Hope and her boyfriend, Fisher, waited by a warm fire. The ocean was tranquil. The moon was full and sparkled on the white sand. A million stars lit up the night sky.

Ransom's mouth fell open. "This is beautiful." He put his arms out and spun in a circle, looking up at the stars. "Are we going swimming?"

"Are you kidding me? This is the Oregon coast, not Hawaii. The ocean is about fifty-two degrees," Sophie said. "We're making s'mores."

"Some what?" Ransom asked.

"S'mores. The best desert on the planet. And if you're lucky, your mallow will be burnt and you will have sand in your chocolate," Sophie said.

"But first," Esther said, "I want to introduce you to Hope and her boyfriend, Fisher. Hope is going to sing to us."

And there under the stars, by the fire, Hope sang all of her favorite Celtic songs. Nephi gave Paisley his jacket to wear, Esther held Parker's hand, and Sophie set marshmallows on fire.

# About the Author

© Photo by Haley Miller Captures

Shannon Symonds lives in a small beach town in Oregon where she works, writes, and runs by the sea. She loves her massive extended family, six children, and, well . . . everyone. She is an expert bonfire builder and s'more maker. She believes we can change the world one heart at a time and every small act makes a difference. Her motto is, "Love really is the answer; it always was, and it always will be."

Scan to visit

https://www.cozymysteriesbythesea.com/